M000033948

THE EGG
THAT WOULDN'T
HATCH

DAPHNE ASHLING PURPUS

Copyright © 2013 Daphne Ashling Purpus
All rights reserved.

ISBN: 0615763308
ISBN-13: 9780615763309
Library of Congress Control Number: 2013902123
Purpus Publishing, Vashon, WA

DEDICATION

This novel is dedicated to my daughter, Pamela; my son, Eric; my granddaughter, Josie; and my sisters, Jan and Stephanie.

CONTENTS

ACKNOWLEDGMENTS

So many people have helped, inspired, and supported me. First I'd like to thank the folks at National Novel Writing Month (NaNoWriMo) for all their encouragement and pep talks. I completed the first draft of *The Egg that Wouldn't Hatch* during the month of November 2012.

Next I'd like to thank the members of my Wednesday bridge class, who have been unfailing in their support of my efforts: Blythe Bartlett, Jude Boardman, Bill Bryce, Tink Campbell, Raynor Christianson, Edna Dam, Jim Dam, Beth de Groen, Barbara Garrison, Billie Hendrix, John McCoy, JoAnn Nielsen, Janet Quimby, Julia Rhoads, Peg Rider, Jerry Snell, Sharon Staehli, Dave Schweinler, Ellen Trout, and Carolyn Youngblood.

I also would like to thank my students—both past and present, at Student Link, Vashon's alternative high school—who continue to inspire me with their drive, determination, maturity, and insight in the face of major adversities. They are the real Dragon Riders.

Finally many thanks (in no particular order) to Cynthia Zheutlin, for her gentle wisdom; Nan Hammett, for her friendship and collegial support; Lydia Schoch, for her empathy and wisdom; Peter Scott, for his interest and encouragement; Kathy

Wheaton, for her friendship; Amber Starcher, for her kindness; Kelly Wright, for her enthusiasm and interest; Nell Coffman and Connie Gaut, for their empathic and knowledgeable care of my fur family; and Anja Moritz, for her wisdom, kind support, and wonderful lunches.

MAP OF THE
FOUR NATIONS

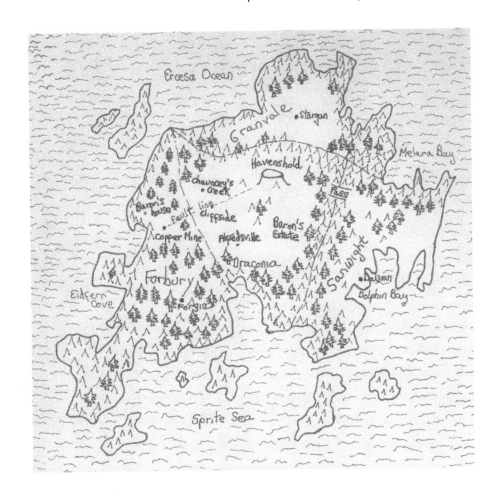

PROLOGUE

Lucy looked up at the clear blue sky as she hurried to her tree house. She wanted to get there before either of her parents thought up something else for her to do. She knew they worked hard to keep the dairy farm running smoothly, and she loved the cows, but right now she had a new book she wanted to read. Seven years old and small for her age, she had hazel eyes, as well as long brown hair that she wore in braided pigtails. She loved to read, and the librarian at her school had found her a new book about animals. She couldn't wait to start it.

Lucy raced up the rickety ladder to her tree house. Her father had built the house for her fifth birthday, and she loved it. It was a bit wobbly in spots, as her father was no carpenter, but that just added charm. Lucy had fixed it up with cozy blankets and pillows, which she certainly would need today, as snow had fallen overnight, but her bright-pink coat was warm, and she had lots of stuffed animals as well.

She made herself comfortable and opened her book. She had read only a page or so when she felt the tree house shake a little. She thought that was odd, but she kept reading. Then she heard her mother shouting for her. Lucy figured it must be something important, as her mother never shouted, but she wanted to finish the page she was on first. It would take only a few minutes.

Lucy read as her mother's shouts became more frantic. Then she noticed the tree was *definitely* moving. She looked down, through the doorway of the tree house, and saw the tree tipping. Lucy became scared. She moved toward the ladder, but instead of reaching the ladder, she tumbled out of the tree house.

Her mother reached her just as Lucy hit the ground. She threw herself on top of her daughter to protect her as the tree and the tree house came crashing down on them.

The next thing Lucy remembered was waking up feeling as if she were flying. She opened her eyes and felt a terrible pain in her right arm. She began to cry. Her father always had told her that big girls don't cry, but she hurt so much. She tried to distract herself by looking around, when suddenly she realized she *was* flying. She was on the back of a purple dragon.

A kind voice said to her, "Don't worry, Lucy. You're safe now. My name is Emily, and this is my dragon, Esmeralda. We're taking you to the hospital at Havenshold."

Lucy lived in a small village named Cliffside that was about halfway between Draconia's capital city, Alfredsville, and the Dragon Riders' home, Havenshold, which was built on and around the nation's volcano. Lucy never had been outside her own village.

Lucy wondered why a dragon and rider were carrying her to the hospital. What had happened? Why did her arm hurt so much? Where were her parents? She then drifted off to sleep again after taking a drink of water from the bottle Emily offered her, unaware that Emily had given her more pain medicine in her water.

When Lucy awoke she was lying in a hospital bed with her right arm completely bandaged. The room was bright and cheerful. There were other beds in the room, but as far as Lucy could tell, they were empty. The door to the room opened, and a young woman walked in. She had long brown braids like Lucy's and kind brown eyes.

"Do you remember me? I'm Emily. Esmeralda and I brought you here. How are you doing?" she asked.

"I don't know," Lucy said. "What happened? Where are my parents? What's wrong with my arm?"

Emily took a deep breath and looked down at the girl. "There was a terrible earthquake," she began. "Where you live was badly damaged. Dragon Riders were called in to help evacuate the wounded."

"What about my parents? Are they all right?" Lucy asked.

Emily hesitated. "Your father's left leg was broken, but it'll heal. He's here at the Havenshold medical facility. He'll be in to see you as soon as he can."

"What about my mom?" Lucy began to cry.

"I'm really sorry, Lucy," Emily said. "She...she died. She put herself between you and the falling tree..." Emily pressed her lips together and smiled a sad smile.

Lucy began to cry in earnest. Emily sat down softly on Lucy's bed and held her.

"I saw her running over to my tree house, and she was calling to me to come down, but I wanted to read one more page. I should have come right away!" Lucy sobbed.

"As bad as this earthquake was," Emily said, "I don't think it would have made a difference. Your mother wanted *you* to live, and you didn't do anything wrong. Remember that."

"What about my arm? Is it broken, like my father's leg?" Lucy asked. Her whole body was shaking, and her mind was all jumbled.

"Your right hand was smashed in the earthquake. Unfortunately they couldn't save it. They had to amputate it just above the wrist. I am *so* very sorry," Emily said, as she softly stroked Lucy's good shoulder.

"But I can feel it! You're wrong!" cried Lucy, looking at her arm. She was shaking harder now.

"I'm sorry, Lucy. That's normal. They call it a phantom feeling, but you *have* lost your hand. We'll do our best to teach you to manage, but you're left-handed, right? That'll make things a bit easier."

Lucy sobbed and turned her face into the pillows.

Emily didn't know what to say. She was only ten years older than Lucy and still in her apprenticeship as a Dragon Rider. Nothing in her life had prepared her to deal with this kind of tragedy. With no words left to say, she silently left Lucy's room.

As Emily left, a tall, heavyset man with graying hair walked in on crutches. With a grimace on his face, he went over to Lucy's bed. "What did I tell you about crying?" he asked her.

She looked up at him and tried to stop crying. "But Mommy's dead...and my hand is gone!" she wailed.

Her father answered, "Well, we'll just have to work that much harder. We're going home. Get your clothes on."

At that moment a nurse came into the room to give Lucy some food. The nurse took one look at Lucy's father, Eugene, and said, "What are you doing out of bed and dressed?"

Eugene said, "I'm here to get my daughter. We're going home. There's lots of work to be done."

The nurse said, "You need to stay here—both of you—for at least a week. Lucy will need physical therapy."

"We aren't staying," Eugene said. "We won't be beholden to Dragon Riders. Where are her clothes?"

The nurse opened a closet and took out Lucy's torn, filthy clothes and tried again to change Eugene's mind. "At least let me get these cleaned up and mended. And you *both* need something to eat."

"We don't need anything from you," Eugene snapped. He took the clothes and threw them onto Lucy's bed. "Get these on." The nurse moved toward Lucy, but Eugene stopped her. "My daughter needs to learn to fend for herself. She might as well start now."

The nurse frowned. "If you insist. I'll go find a doctor to sign your paperwork."

Eugene stared down at Lucy but didn't offer any help as she struggled to get into her clothes. She cried out several times when she bumped her arm. The pain medication was beginning to wear off, and her arm throbbed, but she bit her lip and tried not to cry out.

A doctor came hurrying in, but stopped dead in his track, horrified by the scene in front of him. "Can't I persuade you to stay at least one night?"

"No, you can't," Eugene said. "We need to get home and find our cows. They won't milk themselves."

"The Dragon Riders are out there taking care of the cleanup and looking after folks and their livestock until things return to normal."

"Things won't *ever* return to normal," Eugene snapped back. "And the sooner we get on with life, the better for everyone."

The doctor sighed. "Well, I've prepared a few days' worth of medicine for you both. It's in this bag. Please follow the directions carefully. Lucy especially will be in a lot of pain. You need to watch for swelling or renewed bleeding. The visiting nurse will stop by tomorrow to check on you both."

Lucy and Eugene left the hospital. Eugene asked another dairy farmer to take them home in his wagon. They had to get into the back of the wagon. While the other farmer helped Eugene, Lucy was left to figure out for herself how to get up into the wagon bed. Feeling lost and alone, she realized her life had changed forever.

– 1 –

A NORMAL DAY

Lucy woke up screaming from a nightmare. As with all of her nightmares, she'd been reliving the events of the harrowing earthquake six years earlier. She got out of bed and sat up quietly, hoping she hadn't woken her father. The house was still and quiet. She looked out of her attic bedroom window and saw that dawn wasn't far off. She knew she wouldn't sleep anymore, so she started to get ready for the day.

After washing, getting dressed, and combing her short brown hair, she caught a glimpse of herself in her mirror. She missed her long braids, but more than that, she missed the way her mother had combed and braided her hair every morning. It was their special time together. The earthquake had stolen that. She'd had to have her hair cut short, because she couldn't manage braids one-handed. Besides her missing hand, that was the most visual reminder for her that her childhood had ended in tragedy and far too early.

Lucy climbed down the stairs as quietly as she could and entered the kitchen. She stoked the woodstove, adding more wood from the nearby stack, so it would start to heat the small house. Then she headed out to the barn. Ever since the earthquake, her father had insisted that she feed the cows and also muck out their stalls. She couldn't do the milking. Her father was quick to remind her that her mother always had done half the milking, and now he had to do it all, so at the very least, she could clean the barn and feed the cows.

It was hard work, but it got a bit easier each year as she grew and as she learned how her new body worked. Lucy liked being by herself, so she tried to get out to the barn to do her chores before her father woke. Lucy had always had the ability to sense what animals were feeling, and that ability had grown stronger as she matured. She visited each of the twenty cows her father kept and checked in with them. It wasn't exactly telepathy—at least not how she imagined the riders were with their dragons. The cows didn't talk to her in her head, but she could sense whether they were content. Her father, of course, didn't believe any of this, so Lucy had stopped sharing her thoughts with him. When she discovered that a cow had a sore foot, as had happened last month with Blue Moon, she would find a way either to fix the foot or get her father to look at it by saying she had seen the cow limping.

This morning everything seemed in order, and she mucked out all the stalls, fed everyone—with a little extra treat for Blue Moon, since she was Lucy's favorite—and headed back to the house.

Lucy entered the small kitchen and was glad for the warmth. The winter solstice was still a month away, but this already had proven to be a colder fall than usual. Lucy opened the icebox and took out some eggs for her father's breakfast as well as some cheese for his lunch. Lucy also was responsible for all of their meals. She quickly made sandwiches for lunch—cheese for her father and peanut butter for herself. Her father's lunch went into the icebox, and Lucy put her own into her schoolbag. Next she made coffee for her father and filled a large thermos. She saved the rest for his breakfast. By now she heard her father moving upstairs, so she started to cook breakfast. She had porridge, and she made an omelet for him. She'd gotten the timing down perfectly so that she was sliding the omelet onto his plate as he walked through the door. She poured him a mug of coffee as well, before sitting down to her own breakfast.

Lucy had grown to hate mealtimes. Her father almost never spoke. Since her mother's death, he'd become a recluse. When he did speak, it was to find fault with something Lucy had done, so she dreaded hearing him clear his throat before he began to talk.

This morning was a silent one. Her father wolfed down his food, grabbed his thermos, and headed out to the barn to milk the cows and get on with his day. Lucy breathed more easily once he was out of the house. She quickly cleaned their dishes, made sure everything was spotless, put on her coat, grabbed her schoolbag, and headed outside. She had a two-mile walk to school, but she didn't mind. None of the other schoolchildren lived near her, and she was glad for that.

As she approached the schoolyard, one of the boys, Sam—a large boy, who should have graduated last year but had flunked—started to tease her, calling her "gimp" and "one hand." She ignored him and his friends, who joined in on the teasing. She was used to this and used to the fact that no one would stand up for her. She was in the final grade of the school. From here she would have to find an apprenticeship.

Some of the students, both her age and a year younger, had been selected as candidates for the dragon hatching, which would take place on the winter solstice, but she wasn't surprised that she hadn't been chosen. What dragon would choose a cripple?

Her school days were OK most of the time. Lucy was very bright, which is why she was graduating a year early, and she loved to learn, especially science. Her teacher, Mr. Jones, was kind, but he hovered over her too much, which made the other kids dislike her even more. Still he gave her extra books. She was determined to study volcanology and earthquakes. That's what she wanted to become an apprentice in.

That day, as soon as school was over, Lucy went to the Cliffside Animal Clinic, where she had a part-time job. She loved working with animals, and she was good with them—maybe too good, as she made the head technician, Agnes, jealous. Agnes was a short woman with black hair and nearly black eyes. She almost never smiled, and she seemed to delight in bullying those under her, especially Lucy. Lucy wondered why her own life was so difficult. People seemed to shun her because of her arm, or because she was smart, or because she was just different.

This was Thursday, and it was the vet's surgery day. Dr. Penelope—a short, heavyset woman with short, light-brown hair and green eyes—was a brilliant vet, extremely talented, and loved the challenges of veterinary medicine. She always wanted Lucy to steady the animals while she and Agnes operated, and Agnes hated that. Agnes took sly little digs at Lucy whenever she thought no one else could hear. Lucy had learned that the best thing to do was simply to ignore the comments and stay focused on her work. She really didn't understand why Agnes worked here. She was dreadful with animals. She was a competent technician when the animals were asleep, but the minute they woke up, Agnes was either terrified of them or bored with them. She treated them badly, ignored them, and refused to show them any compassion or sympathy.

What Lucy found to be even more amazing was that Dr. Penelope thought Agnes was the very best. Agnes was her favorite tech, and Lucy couldn't understand why. Couldn't Dr. Penelope see that Agnes bullied the rest of the staff? Agnes was as bad as Sam at school.

Today's surgery involved cleaning the teeth of a very old dog. Lucy made sure she stayed in contact with the dog throughout the procedure, comforting him and sending calming thoughts his way, as Agnes scraped and scraped at the tartar until the poor dog's gums were bleeding. Lucy felt so sorry for him. Dr. Penelope also had to pull ten teeth, which would leave him with a very sore mouth.

When they were done, Lucy placed the dog in a kennel and made sure he was covered with a blanket and had water. Once the dog started to wake, Lucy was there to comfort him. Later, when his owner came, Lucy helped the dog out of his kennel, because Agnes had magically disappeared. Agnes hated getting dogs out of kennels.

Finally Lucy's shift at the clinic was over, and she walked the two miles back home. She still had to do the evening rounds in the barn, make dinner, and do her homework before she could go to bed. She just hoped that her father had had a reasonable day, or the evening would be even more miserable.

As she was walking home, Lucy allowed herself to think about Emily, the woman who had saved her life. She wondered how she and Esmeralda were doing. Her father had banned them both from the farm shortly after the accident, and that had hurt Lucy a lot. Emily was so kind. Lucy would have liked to just sit and talk with her.

She knew that Emily and Esmeralda had graduated from their apprenticeship three years ago, and occasionally Lucy caught a glimpse of purple in the sky as they flew overhead. That made Lucy feel a bit better. Maybe they were watching out for her despite her father. Lucy thought about the upcoming hatching and how wonderful it would have been if she'd been chosen as a candidate for a dragon egg. Then she shook her head and scolded herself. *Stop thinking about things that can never be,* she told herself, as the small dairy farm came into view.

— 2 —
THE CLINIC

It was Saturday morning, and Lucy had to get through her chores quickly, because she was working a full day at Cliffside Animal Clinic. She'd had to tell her father at breakfast that Blue Moon had a blocked teat, and he hadn't believed her. "Don't you think I'd notice if a cow wasn't firing on all cylinders?" he had yelled.

She had the sense not to answer, but a little while later, her father came storming in, wanting to know what he was supposed to do about a blocked teat. He hadn't taken kindly to Lucy's answer that he needed to get a vet out to treat it.

"Haven't you learned anything in all the time you've worked there? What good are you anyway?" he screamed as he left the kitchen, slamming the door behind him.

Lucy knew he had gotten her the job at the clinic with the hope that eventually she would become apprenticed to Dr. Penelope, and he'd have free vet services for his cows. He really didn't care that she wanted to be either a volcanologist or a geologist. Lucy had been helping out at the clinic for several years, and while she enjoyed it—at least when Agnes wasn't around—it wasn't what she wanted to do for the rest of her life.

Lucy arrived at the clinic. She told Marta, who scheduled appointments, that her dad needed a farm visit. Marta rolled her eyes. No one wanted to go out to Lucy's farm and deal with Eugene, but there weren't any other options. Lucy loved Marta, who was gentle and a bit heavyset with short gray hair. Marta always kept an eye out for her, and Lucy appreciated it. Lucy knew that Marta would have liked to mother her, but she also knew her father wouldn't allow that.

Lucy went into the back room, which the clinic used as an operating room, a kennel for small animals, and anything else they needed to keep the general public away from. Dr. Penelope called her over immediately. She was doing an emergency cesarean on a small dog that had a dead puppy blocking her birth canal. The dog was in obvious distress, and Agnes was trying to sedate her, but the dog kept snapping at her hand.

Agnes yelled, "This dog is impossible to work on!"

Lucy walked over and gently placed her hand on the dog's head, as she sang and talked to her softly. Immediately the dog calmed down. Lucy let the dog know they were all trying to help her deliver her puppies. As the dog grew calmer, Agnes managed to sedate her, and Dr. Penelope began the cesarean.

All of a sudden, there was blood everywhere. Dr. Penelope yelled at Lucy, "You clumsy fool! Where's the clamp I asked for? Why do you *always* drop things? Agnes is right—you *are* the most incompetent fool."

Lucy was thunderstruck. She could tell Dr. Penelope was having a bad day, and when Dr. Penelope had a bad day, it was a bad day for everyone. However, Lucy rarely had been singled out like this. What did she mean by she '*always* dropped things'? Lucy was extra careful, because she only had one hand. She never dropped things. Did *everyone* at the clinic hate her?

Dr. Penelope got the bleeding under control, but she kept right on ripping into Lucy, calling her names and repeating what Agnes obviously had told her. Dr. Penelope accused her of every kind of incompetence, from botching the recordkeeping to failing to obey orders.

Lucy didn't move. She tried hard not to listen to the tirade. She needed to stay calm for the sake of the pregnant dog.

As soon as the cesarean was finished—with three live, healthy puppies—Lucy fled outside, crying her heart out. Marta followed her out. Everyone in the clinic, staff and patients alike, had heard the explosion. Marta came over to Lucy and said, "Please don't cry. You know what Dr. Penelope's like when she's upset. That dog is the family pet for a *very* important client. And we all know what Agnes is like. She makes up gossip and spreads it as far as she can. She used to be a vet before she lost her license, so she thinks she's better than everyone else here."

"I know," sobbed Lucy, "but I didn't drop anything, and if I hadn't calmed down the poor little mother dog, Agnes wouldn't have been able to sedate her. Why can't anyone see how bad Agnes is with animals? She doesn't care about them at all. She doesn't watch over them as they wake up after surgery. She doesn't help them or soothe them. I watched her the other day trying to get a dog out of a kennel, and she just snatched at him, trying to grab his collar and drag him out. She never thinks about how the animal might feel. That dog was scared and hurting, but Agnes didn't care."

"You're right," Marta said, "and Agnes is jealous of *you,* because you're so good with animals. Agnes makes up lies and then spreads them to Dr. Penelope, who just takes her word for everything, because she doesn't have the time, energy, or inclination to discover the truth."

"It isn't right! If Dr. Penelope had a problem with me, she shouldn't have yelled at me in front of everyone," Lucy said.

Marta put her arms around Lucy. "I know, hon," she said soothingly. "None of this is right. I'm so sorry. You know that Dr. Penelope will never apologize, don't you?" Lucy nodded. Marta continued, "You'll be graduating in a few months, and then you can apply for that internship you want with Gregory, that sweet Emily's boyfriend. My bet is that he'll take you. You're bright and eager, and he's looking for more volcanologists. I don't know why no one seems to want to study volcanoes and earthquakes, given that we live right next to a live volcano, but I know *you* do, and Gregory would be lucky to get you. So, please, try to hang on for a bit longer. It'll all work out."

"But everyone heard what she said," wailed Lucy. "What will they think of me? If these lies spread, especially when everyone looks at me as a cripple anyway, how will I ever get away from the dairy farm and find an apprenticeship? It's all so awful."

"Hush, there. You know that everyone knows how difficult Dr. Penelope can be on her bad days. There's no one more skilled than she is as a vet, but there are also very few people who have such awful people skills. We all know that, and we all know there isn't a grain of truth in anything Agnes spreads. If the staff didn't need their jobs so badly, they'd stand up in unison, and then something would have to happen. Instead Agnes is able to pick them off one by one. But please realize that no one is going to believe these lies about you, and soon you'll be out of here. Just hang on for a little longer."

Lucy was grateful for Marta's words. Some days it seemed as if everyone was against her, but Marta always had a kind word for her. Lucy tried a tentative smile. "If Dr. Penelope thinks her day is bad now, wait until she has to deal with my father and the blocked teat in his number-one milking cow!"

"That's the spirit," Marta said. "And one day Dr. Penelope will realize why she has such a high staff turnover. We're just going to have to rise above her bullying and Agnes's bullying and turn away from their wrath with kindness."

"I am so sick of bullies," Lucy said, thinking about Agnes, her father, Sam, and the other bullies at school.

Marta and Lucy headed back inside. Lucy washed her face in the restroom and went to look after the new mom and her puppies. The morning passed without any other emergencies. After lunch, Dr. Penelope came over to Lucy and said, "Well, we'd better head out to your place and check on that cow your father's worried about."

Lucy nodded. Marta was right. Dr. Penelope did what she wanted and took no prisoners. If she didn't like something, she exploded, ripping into whatever unfortunate person was in her wake. No wonder Agnes felt free to do the same. There was a big difference, however, between the two women. Agnes was determined to undermine everyone, holding grudges and spreading malicious gossip. Dr. Penelope had a good heart, and she loved animals. She had a very quick temper, but once she blew up, she forgot all about it. Lucy thought it might be an interesting experience to watch Dr. Penelope and her father, who also had a vicious temper and no kind words for anyone.

— 3 —

THE MOST HORRENDOUS DAY

Lucy woke up late on Monday morning, and that was never good. It took her longer to get ready than most people, and whenever she hurried, she ended up dropping things and being a lot clumsier. She tried to hurry anyway and decided she wouldn't pick up her room or make her bed, since her father never came up to her small attic bedroom anyway.

Racing down the stairs, she glanced quickly at the door to her father's room to see that it was still shut. *At least he isn't up yet,* she thought, as she raced through the kitchen and out to the barn.

She grabbed a rake and began to muck out the stalls. In her rush she dropped the rake several times. She thought she'd gotten pretty clever at pulling the rake with her left hand while using her right stump to balance it, but hurrying wasn't helping her.

Lucy started to breathe faster. She just had to be done before her father came out, or he would be really mad. He needed the stables cleaned and the cows fed before he came in for the milking, and she still had his breakfast to make. Obviously she would be going without, but he wouldn't stand for not having his eggs in the morning.

Lucy tossed hay into the bins for the cows and raced back to the kitchen. *Oh, no,* she thought. *How could I have forgotten to light the stove?* Tears ran down her cheeks, but she quickly wiped them away as she lit the fire. It took several tries before it caught. *Will nothing go right?* she wondered, as she looked around the dingy kitchen. *Things were never this bad when Mother was alive. Oh, why couldn't I have come faster? It's my fault that she's dead.*

Lucy felt she should have been able to prevent her mother's death and her father's misery. Her father had been a good and happy man most of the time when her mother had been alive. He seemed to love Lucy and liked making her things in his precious spare time, like her tree house, but now he was an angry, bitter man, and no matter what Lucy did, she couldn't make him happy.

She grabbed the breakfast things first. *I can make our lunches while he eats breakfast*, she told herself. The stove wasn't as hot as she liked, so she decided the eggs would have to be scrambled. That was another strike against her, as her father liked scrambled eggs less than any other kind. She could add some toast, and she had the coffee going.

Her father was coming down the stairs, and Lucy hurried to get his plate on the table. All of a sudden, just as her father entered the kitchen, the plate slipped through her fingers and smashed on the brick floor. Scrambled eggs flew everywhere.

Her father looked at the mess. "What am I supposed to eat now?"

Lucy started to cry.

"Don't you start your bawling," he said with a scowl. "You're worthless! You can't even make breakfast without causing a mess. A worthless cripple—that's all you are." He grabbed his coffee thermos and stormed out of the kitchen, slamming the door behind him.

Lucy bent down to clean up the mess. *He's right,* she thought as she worked. *I'm worthless, and it's my fault that we're in this mess.*

As soon as the floor was clean, Lucy set to work to make his lunch. She didn't have time to do hers, but she wasn't hungry. She tried to make an extra-tasty lunch, hoping it would make up for the morning disaster. Just as she was finishing, she heard her father scream from the barn. *Oh, no, what have I done now?* she thought, as she ran out to the barn.

Her father was waving a piece of paper. "What is this bill all about?"

Lucy had forgotten that the clinic had given her the bill for the farm visit on Saturday. It must have fallen out of her pocket when she was feeding the cows. "The clinic asked me to give this to you. It's for unblocking Blue Moon's teat on Saturday."

"I know what it says, but why are we paying? I thought you worked there. Isn't it enough that I allow that? Shouldn't I get some consideration for letting you work?" Her father was getting redder and redder in the face, and he was snapping his words out.

"They gave you the employee discount," Lucy said, but before she could explain any further, he slapped her across the face.

"Don't you talk back to me. What business do you have taking their side?" he snarled.

Lucy looked down at the dirt floor and muttered, "Sorry." He didn't hit her often, but when he did, it was bad.

"Well, you take this back to them and let them know I'm not paying it. I deserve better than this." He shoved the bill into Lucy's hand and stormed off.

As soon as he turned his back, Lucy raced out of the barn with tears streaming down her face. She darted into the kitchen long enough to grab her backpack then ran the first part of the two miles to school. *Can this day get any worse?* she thought.

She managed to get to school just as the bell rang and took her seat. Mr. Jones asked the students to take out their math books. As soon as Lucy opened her desk, she realized the day had just gotten a lot worse. She looked around and saw Sam and his buddies smirking. Her desk was filled with honey. It covered her books and was beginning to drip to the floor. She quickly closed the lid.

Mr. Jones asked everyone to turn to page 145 and to do the problems in the first set. He quickly noticed that Lucy didn't have her book out. He walked to her desk to see what was wrong. Lucy silently opened the lid.

Mr. Jones looked very sad with his mouth turning down at the corners as he said, "How did this happen?"

Lucy sat there, realizing that if she blamed anyone, she would have even bigger problems. "Maybe something leaked from my lunch." Lucy didn't even like honey.

Mr. Jones said, "Well, you'll have to replace all these books."

"Yes, sir," replied Lucy.

"You can clean this up during lunch," he began, and Lucy was glad she hadn't bothered to make herself any lunch. "In the meantime," he continued, "get another math book and any of the others that are damaged off the shelf, and sit in the empty desk at the end of the row. I'll total a bill for you to take home tonight."

"Yes, sir," Lucy said very softly. She knew what her father would say about this. Thank heavens she had some of her books in her backpack, all the ones she had needed for last night's homework. She vowed that from now on she would keep everything with her.

The class settled down to work, and Lucy avoided looking at Sam. Lunchtime was long and hard. At least she knew a lot about cleaning, since she had to do so much of it at home, but still she'd barely finished when the afternoon classes resumed.

Finally the bell rang, and Lucy went to get her backpack so she could load it up, but even that was not to be. Some-one—*And I know just who,* thought Lucy—had cut the straps. Fortunately the culprit had left the interior undamaged, so she was able to put all her books and school stuff into it. It was very hard for her to carry one-handed. She had to balance it on her right arm and grip it with her left hand. She finally managed to get her coat on, her backpack in hand, and the bill for the honey-damaged books in her pocket and headed out to work at the clinic.

Marta took one look at Lucy as she walked through the clinic door and jumped up from her desk to help her. "You look like you've had a really rough day," Marta said, as she took Lucy's backpack from her.

"It's been the second worst day of my life," Lucy said.

"Oh, dear. Can I help?"

"Not really," Lucy moaned, "unless you can work miracles. I gave my father his vet bill, and he flat out *refused* to pay it. He says he should get free services because I work here." She handed Marta the bill.

"Oh, hon," Marta said. "You shouldn't have to deal with this. I'll pass it on to Dr. Penelope, and she can handle it. Don't you worry at all."

"He's going to flip when I give him the bill for my books that were destroyed when someone poured *honey* into my desk," continued Lucy, tears welling in her eyes.

Marta patted her shoulder and shook her head. "That's ter-rible."

Just then Dr. Penelope stormed into the reception area, looking for Lucy. "Did you do this?" she demanded, waving a piece of paper in front of Lucy.

"Do what?" Lucy said.

"It's the wrong prescription for yesterday's emergency. Agnes said she gave the instructions to you, and *you* filled it wrong. How could you do that?" asked Dr. Penelope, who didn't notice how upset Lucy already was.

"I didn't work yesterday," Lucy said quietly.

"Well, I meant Saturday, when we had that cesarean. This pain medication dosage is for a much larger dog. It's lucky Agnes caught it, or the dog might have died."

"I didn't make up the prescription. Agnes just handed me a bottle and told me to give it to the owners," answered Lucy.

"Don't lie!" yelled Dr. Penelope. "Agnes would *never* do such a thing!"

That was the last straw for poor Lucy. She grabbed her backpack off Marta's desk before racing out the door. She kept right on running for as long as she could.

Where can I go? she thought, as she slowed to a walk. *I sure can't go home.* Then she remembered a cave up in the hills that she'd found last summer. *That's where I'll go,* she decided, as she headed away from town.

— 4 —
THE CAVE

Lucy hung onto her backpack and climbed. She fell a number of times, but she was determined to make it. The path was steep, and it was hard to keep her balance with the backpack, but she needed it. The skills she'd developed over the past six years of her young life stood her in good stead now.

After about an hour of hiking, Lucy stopped and sat on a rock. She looked back at the village. She saw her school and the clinic, and she knew her father's farm was off in the distance, just out of sight. Soon her father would come in for the evening, and he would expect his supper to be cooked and ready. *Well, not tonight,* thought Lucy, as she stood up and hiked higher into the hills.

It was dark when Lucy finally reached the cave. She went inside and collapsed on the cave floor. She was so glad she had found this place last summer. She had no idea what she would do now. She was only thirteen and too young to make it on her own. On the other hand, she'd been doing her mother's work for a number of years. She'd taken over much of a wife's work even before her mother's funeral. She hadn't been able to do much at that age, but that didn't stop her father from expecting her to cook and clean.

That meant she had a lot of domestic skills. She wondered whether she could go to another village and get hired as a maid or something. As soon as she thought that, she told herself, *Father's right. No one would hire a cripple.*

Lucy lay down on the floor and pulled her coat over her. She emptied some of the books out of her backpack to make a pillow. It wasn't a very satisfactory one, but it was better than nothing. She was so tired. She started to sob uncontrollably. How would she manage? She was scared and alone. She knew on some level that she deserved everything she got, because she had caused her mother's death, but even so, she just couldn't handle it. She hadn't had anything to eat all day, but she couldn't find anything in the dark, so she fell asleep from exhaustion.

Tossing and turning, she had one nightmare after another. Her nightmares seemed to mix the day's events with the earthquake.

She was falling from a tree, but then she landed in a vat of honey and was drowning.

Her mother was calling to her, holding up a tree and urging her to run.

Her father was yelling at her about the bill for her mother's funeral.

Lucy cried out in her sleep. She couldn't make herself wake up. Suddenly someone was holding her, rubbing her shoulders, and murmuring comforting words. Lucy woke. Emily and Esmeralda were in the cave with her. It was good that the cave was so large, as Esmeralda was fully grown.

Lucy sat up and said, "What are you two doing here?"

Emily said, "We were flying overhead when we heard your nightmares. You have a strong psychic presence. Did you know that?" Emily was asking more as a way to distract Lucy from her obvious terror.

Lucy shrugged, still groggy. "I can sense what animals are feeling, but my father says that's rubbish."

"What are you doing out here all by yourself?" Emily asked.

Lucy looked down at the cave floor. "I've done everything wrong. My father is furious with me. I'm sure I've been fired from the animal clinic. And I can't stand to go back to school."

Emily looked at Esmeralda, who sent her thoughts telepathically to Emily. *This young girl is carrying too big a burden. Remember when we rescued her from the earthquake? Why wouldn't her father let us help? She's really suffering.*

Emily sent own her thoughts back to Esmeralda. *I've tried to find out about her, especially after the baron's war ended, but her father won't let any Dragon Riders anywhere near them.* Emily turned to Lucy and said, "Why don't you tell us what brought you here?"

Lucy started to cry again. "I spilled my father's breakfast on the floor, and then he wouldn't pay the vet bill for fixing Blue Moon's teat, and the bullies at school poured honey in my desk and ruined most of my books, which means my father will have to pay for new ones, and then those bullies cut the straps on my backpack, and Dr. Penelope yelled at me for a prescription error that *wasn't* mine—Agnes did it and then blamed me, but Dr. Penelope won't hear anything said against Agnes—and I just couldn't take it anymore, so I *ran away!*" she said in an explosive rush of words. Her sobs took over again.

Emily held her for the longest time as she tried to figure out what to do. The cave was very cold by now, so Emily had Esmeralda light a fire from some wood someone had left in the cave. Emily looked through her saddlebags, hoping to find that she still had some food. She and Esmeralda had been on patrol all day, but they weren't expected back until tomorrow afternoon, so Emily decided to stay put in the cave with Lucy. She made things as comfortable as she could and even found a dinner pack to heat up. As soon as it was ready, she said, "Shall we have something to eat?"

"Please," Lucy said. "I didn't get anything to eat today. I had to clean up the mess I made of my father's breakfast and then race to school without a lunch, which I couldn't have eaten anyway, because I had to clean the honey out of my desk, and then I ran away from the clinic and came here, and by then it was dark."

"Oh," Emily said. "It really isn't so late. You know it gets dark really early this time of year. It's only about ten o'clock. Let's have some food together, and then we'll bed down for the night. I have more blankets, and Esmeralda will tend the fire. She'll also chase away any nightmares you might have. How does that sound?"

Lucy looked at Esmeralda. "Can you really do that?"

Esmeralda honored Lucy by answering. *I can for you. I'm happy to help!*

"I could hear her in my head!" Lucy exclaimed to Emily. "With the animals I work with, I only get a sense of what they're feeling but no real words."

Emily smiled. "Not everyone can hear telepathic speech." Lucy smiled back.

As they ate dinner, Lucy told Emily about everything that had happened since the earthquake. Emily's heart broke as she realized that, thanks to Lucy's father, no one had been allowed to help Lucy—either with the physical challenge of the missing hand, or with therapy to deal with the earthquake and her mother's death. Lucy, though strong, had reached her breaking point.

Emily told some stories about life as a Dragon Rider and life at Havenshold, where the dragons, riders, and support community lived. She settled Lucy into her own bedroll and crawled in beside her to be sure she didn't have any more nightmares. She kept telling stories until Lucy fell into a deep sleep.

What are we going to do? We can't let her go back to her father, Emily said to Esmeralda.

Definitely not! That man should be taken and whipped. Esmeralda allowed a deep, low growl to emanate from her belly to emphasize her point.

Well, I imagine he's hurting too, but I agree. He's abused Lucy, and that can't continue.

She would have made a fine Dragon Rider, if it weren't for her hand, Esmeralda thought.

Emily answered, *She's very courageous and resourceful. That's for sure. Tomorrow we're going to talk to her father and get Lucy out of there and up to Havenshold. Any ideas how we might accomplish that?*

I bet Lucy could be "bought," Esmeralda thought. *It sounds to me as if her father only wants a servant.*

As Emily fell asleep, she replied, *Something will come to us. It always does. Thanks for keeping watch. Hopefully tomorrow will be the start of a new life for Lucy.*

— 5 —

THE NEW APPRENTICE

Emily woke up before Lucy. She thought she had a plan, but she needed to contact her brother, Hans, the head of the Dragon Riders. Using Esmeralda to strengthen the telepathic communication, she managed to contact his orange dragon, Fire Dancer, and through Fire Dancer, Hans himself. She told them both what she and Esmeralda had found. She presented her plan, and Hans agreed immediately. Hans was a kind, gentle man and was just as horrified as Emily had been by what had happened to Lucy.

After Emily found some food for breakfast, she woke Lucy. "Time for breakfast. Then we'll go see your father."

Lucy panicked. "No, you *mustn't* come to our farm. Father has threatened to shoot dragons on sight if they land on his property."

"Don't worry," Emily said. "We'll make sure that doesn't happen. I want to talk to your father about *you.* Would you like an apprenticeship at Havenshold, working with our animals? You could finish school there."

"Oh, I'd *love* that...but my father has already said he won't pay for my apprenticeship anywhere. Besides, no one would want a cripple like me." Lucy sighed and stopped eating her breakfast.

"Balderdash," Emily said. "You'll be a real asset at Havens-hold. Trust me! Now finish your breakfast and let's get going. Would you like to ride Esmeralda?"

Lucy's eyes lit up. "Oh, could I? I've always dreamed of being a Dragon Rider. Riding a dragon has to be the best thing in the world."

Emily smiled. "Let's get outside, and I'll lift you up onto Esmeralda's back."

They packed up all their belongings, and Emily stashed Lucy's backpack into one of Esmeralda's saddlebags. She told Lucy exactly where to grab onto Esmeralda with her left hand as she lifted Lucy high up onto Esmeralda's back. Emily quickly stepped onto Esmeralda's bent front leg and vaulted up behind Lucy. "OK," Emily said. "Let's go *tame* your father." Esmeralda soared into the air.

Lucy was overjoyed. She couldn't believe how wonderful it was to be up high on the back of a dragon. *Especially one as gorgeous as Esmeralda,* she thought.

She was surprised when Esmeralda thought back, *Why, thank you, Lucy. You'll make me blush!*

Emily told Esmeralda to take the scenic route so Lucy could have a really good ride before they had to face her father, but all too soon, they had to come down. They landed in front of Lucy's home just as her father came out, waving a shotgun and telling them to get off his land.

Emily vaulted down from Esmeralda but left Lucy seated on Esmeralda's back. "Eugene," she said, "I'm here to ask if you'll allow Lucy to come to Havenshold as an apprentice."

"What?" he shouted. "No! No one would want a crippled, use-less girl like her, and I have no time for dragons either. Besides, I need her here. No one else will have her, but I need someone to cook and clean for me now that her mother is dead." He looked up at Lucy. "Where were you last night? The stables need mucking out, the cows need feeding, and I haven't had my breakfast. You get down here right now and get to work. No school for you today. You'll stay here and make up the work you didn't do yesterday. Don't you ever pull a stunt like this again, or I'll whip you."

Esmeralda roared, sending a jet of flame within inches of Lucy's father. He jumped back and raised his shotgun. Esmeralda lifted her front leg and batted the shotgun clear across the yard. As Lucy's father started to go get it, Emily said, "I'd leave that alone if I were you. Esmeralda doesn't approve of whipping *children*. Now let's talk about that apprenticeship."

"If you think I'm paying any of my hard-earned money for an apprenticeship for her," he shouted as he glared at Lucy, "you're sadly mistaken! She's responsible for my wife's death, and she'll pay for that by doing what I tell her to do."

Emily was appalled. How could Lucy have endured all this and still be as sweet and loving as she was? She continued, "I was here that day, Eugene. You seem to have forgotten that. I heard your wife's last words as Esmeralda and I pulled the tree off her. She asked us to *save Lucy*. That was all she cared about. You should be ashamed."

"If that ungrateful child had come when her mother first had called, the tree wouldn't have hit either of them," Eugene ranted, his face red and drops of white saliva sticking to the corners of his mouth.

"What child ever comes the first time she's called? The tree house started to come apart before the tree fell. Didn't you build the tree house? Maybe it was your fault. Did you ever think of that? Or maybe it was just a tragic accident. Your wife chose to save Lucy with her last breath. Shouldn't you honor that?"

"You're twisting everything around. I don't have a wife, and it's *her fault!*" he shouted, as he pointed to Lucy.

"Maybe. Maybe not," Emily said. "The earthquake could have killed her anyway. It could have killed all three of you. We saw the damage. It was a miracle that you and Lucy survived at all."

"That doesn't change the fact that I need Lucy. You can't have her. I'm not paying for any apprenticeship." He moved toward Esmeralda, as if he were going to drag Lucy down from her back.

"What if *we* paid *you?*" Emily asked softly.

Eugene stopped dead in his tracks. "What do you mean? Apprenticeships are bought by the parents."

Emily continued, "The usual practice is for parents to find someone suitable to train their son or daughter after the child finishes school at fourteen, and then the parents pay that person for a seven-year apprenticeship, but we do things differently at Havenshold. We don't accept money or goods for any of our apprentices."

Eugene said, "How is that possible? Who pays for their school? Their meals?"

"Havenshold is self-sufficient. We pay our own way. When we find suitable people for our support community, we pay them a good wage and provide food and lodging as well. Lucy has a real way with animals and would be a major asset to our animal clinic. She has several years training already, and I know she would enjoy the work and do a good job for us."

"This isn't about what Lucy might *enjoy.* Life isn't about enjoyment. It's about hard work and getting through each day. My answer is no. Lucy, get down here and get to work."

Emily put her hand up. "Stay right where you are, Lucy. Eugene, I know it'll be hard to lose Lucy's services, but in special circumstances like these, we're willing to alter our usual practice and instead pay *you* a fee for your daughter's apprenticeship."

Eugene's eyes lit up. "What kind of fee?"

"Shall we say that we will give you an amount equal to what your dairy farm makes in...three years? That way you could easily hire a servant to help you out," answered Emily.

"Three years? But her apprenticeship would last seven before she could come back. What am I to do for the other four years? And she hasn't even graduated from school yet. She has another year."

"Please don't get greedy. You know full well that my offer is exceedingly generous. Lucy will finish her schooling at Havenshold, working a part-time apprenticeship until she has met the graduation requirements, after which she will get to pick a full apprenticeship in a field of her choice. Shall we step inside and draw up a contract? You can show me your account books, and I'll write you a draft here and now for the full amount as soon as you sign the papers granting Havenshold guardianship over Lucy."

Eugene thought for a few moments, but he obviously knew he'd never get a better offer. He nodded and moved toward the front door.

Emily looked up at Lucy. "Give me your hand, and I'll get you down. You can get any of your things that you want while I sort out the paperwork. Esmeralda will be able to carry anything you'd like to bring with you."

After Lucy climbed down, she looked fearfully toward her house. Emily took her left hand in hers, and together they walked inside. Lucy ran for her bedroom as Emily moved into the kitchen with her father.

Lucy took a look around her room—a room she had lived in for most of her life. What would she want? She looked at her unmade bed and realized she wanted her quilt, because her mother had made it. It had fabrics with animals on them, lots of purple, her favorite color, and a soft purple flannel back. Her mother had stitched her name and loving words in it when she quilted it for Lucy's sixth birthday. Then she gathered up her books and stuffed animals. Maybe she was too old for the stuffed animals, but she couldn't bear to part with them. She brought her few clothes, even though Emily had assured her she wouldn't need them, and she packed up her old hair ribbons, because they bound her to her mother too.

It didn't take Lucy long to pack her few belongings. She put them all inside the quilt and folded them up into a bundle. Just as she was going to try to lift it and realized it was bigger than she'd thought, Emily walked in stuffing some papers into her coat pocket and looking very pleased. "Is this what you want to take?" Emily asked, as she pointed to the folded quilt on the unmade bed.

"Yes," Lucy said. "If it isn't too much."

"Not even close," Emily said with a smile. "Let's get out of here, shall we?"

Lucy nodded and followed her out of the tiny room.

When they got downstairs, Lucy's father had to get in the last word. "When they find out how useless you are, don't think you can come crawling back here!" he barked, as they made their way out the front door.

Emily and Lucy didn't say a word, but Esmeralda sent a thought to both of them. *If Lucy is so "useless," how come he wanted her so much?*

Lucy and Emily both smiled. Soon Lucy was up on Esmeralda again, with Emily sitting behind her, and they were soaring away from Cliffside and all the horrors Lucy had known there.

— 6 —
A TRIP TO THE CAPITAL

As soon as they were in the air, Emily said to Lucy, "We still have a couple of stops to make before we leave Cliffside, don't we?" She felt Lucy stiffen in front of her.

"Yeah, I suppose. I have to return those schoolbooks, or my father will get charged, and I need to let the clinic know I won't be back," Lucy said with a groan.

"I know it'll be hard, but it's the right thing to do. First how about a trip to the capital city, Alfredsville? I have to drop off some papers. That was where we were heading when we picked up your distress call."

"Oh, I'm sorry!" Lucy said. "I didn't mean to be a bother."

"You are *not* a bother. I'm so happy we were in the right place at the right time, and I'm very sorry you had to suffer for so long before we got there. Besides, you'll love the palace, and Clotilda is really delightful."

"Clotilda? You mean *Queen* Clotilda?" Lucy asked in an awe-struck voice.

Emily laughed. "Yep! She doesn't let riders call her 'Queen.' She never wanted to be queen in the first place. To tell you the truth, I think she hates most of it, but she knows we need her. Anyway, it'll be a pleasant excursion. And after I take care of business and we have a lovely lunch, you'll be in much better shape to face the finality of leaving Cliffside."

"OK," Lucy said. "Anything to delay that moment!"

"Look out, palace! Here we come," Emily said, as they soared higher in the sky.

While they were flying, Emily and Esmeralda made telepathic communication with Clotilda and her dragon, Matilda, alerting them to Lucy's situation. Clotilda listened to Emily's account, and then thought back, *I really can't believe this kind of thing is happening in Draconia! I am so happy you found and rescued her. Please come as quickly as you can so I can help sort this out.* Emily agreed.

Lucy watched as the countryside sped by, trying to see in all directions at once. As they neared Alfredsville, Lucy saw tall spires on some buildings, and then lots of houses and streets, laid out like a checkerboard. She couldn't believe how many buildings there were. Cliffside only had one main road and no more than a dozen buildings with houses and farms scattered in the outlying areas. *What a lot of people must live here,* she thought as they flew over the city.

Soon they were landing in the palace courtyard. Lucy looked around, her mouth gaping. She quickly closed her mouth, but her hazel eyes got bigger.

Esmeralda spoke gently to her. *Don't worry. You're safe here, and everyone is very friendly. Just enjoy the visit.*

"Thanks, Esmeralda," Lucy whispered back, as Emily helped her dismount.

Lucy noticed a tall, slim woman with gray hair and steel-blue eyes heading toward them. She had a big smile on her face. As soon as Emily had Lucy on the ground, Emily ran over and gave her a huge hug. "Clotilda! I want you to meet a new friend of mine." They walked to Esmeralda and Lucy.

Clotilda smiled and said gently, "Welcome, Lucy. We're so glad you were able to come here with Emily."

Lucy blushed. She didn't know what to say. First Emily had called her a friend—no one ever had called her that except Marta—and then the queen had said she was *happy* Lucy was here. Lucy's whole world was upside-down. It gave her a warm feeling in the pit of her stomach. She smiled and bobbed her head.

"Come on, you two," Clotilda said, as she put an arm around each of them. She called back over her shoulder, "Matilda is out in the fields if you want to have a visit too, Esmeralda."

Esmeralda took off, sending thoughts to Lucy. *Have fun, you hear?*

Lucy giggled.

As soon as they reached Clotilda's private quarters, she said, "Would you two like to freshen up?"

"Oh, yes," Emily replied. "We spent last night in a cave, and a hot soak would be wonderful! Come on, Lucy. I'll show you."

They walked down a long corridor lined with paintings. Lucy's feet sank into a thick plush carpet, the likes of which she never had seen or felt before. Emily opened a door and said, "I think you'll like this bath."

Lucy looked hesitantly into the room. A very large tub with enormous handles stood at one end. There also was a purple-tiled countertop with a big sink. On another counter with a mirror above it were stacks of purple towels and jars with beads inside. In the corner there was a divided space with a toilet discreetly hidden.

"I've never seen anything like this," Lucy said in a whisper. "We only have an outhouse, and we wash in a basin. The water is pretty cold this time of year, but my father thinks it's nonsense to heat water for bathing. In the summer I can swim in the creek, but most of the time, I just use the basin in my room. Do you have a bath like this where you live?"

Emily smiled. "Yes, in Havenshold all the homes have indoor baths. It's one of the advantages of living up close and personal with the volcano. The Dragon Riders have a hot spring that's big enough for riders and dragons. We're spoiled." She sighed. "Now come on. Let's get you situated here."

A young girl came in. "Clotilda thought Lucy might like some assistance, so she sent me along to show her how everything works. My name is May, and I'd love to help."

"Super," Emily said. "I'll be next door in the blue bath if you need anything."

May ushered Lucy into the purple bathroom and closed the door. May was short, with blonde hair and blue eyes. She appeared to be about Lucy's age. As soon as the door closed, May gushed. "You got to *ride* on a *dragon!* And not just any dragon, but Esmeralda! Wow! Aren't you lucky?"

Lucy was a bit taken aback, but the smile on May's face let her know that May meant no harm. She smiled and nodded. She'd never been *lucky.* May kept right on chattering like a little bird, explaining what everything was and then asking what scent of bath salts Lucy wanted. Lucy was startled, so May opened each jar in turn and let Lucy take a whiff. All the salts were wonderful, but her favorite was the lavender. It reminded her of her mother.

"Lavender it is," said May. "Now just slip out of your clothes while I turn on the taps. You can put your clothes in that bin over there so they can get washed while you soak."

Lucy did as told and soon was happily soaking in lavender bubbles in water that was delightfully hot.

May brought over some shampoos and said, "We have a wonderful lavender shampoo that would go well with the salts. Would you like to try it?"

Lucy nodded, unsure what to say or what would happen next. May went on, "Most folks say I give a wonderful scalp massage, and they want me to wash their hair every time they visit at the palace. May I?"

Lucy smiled. "That would be fun...and Esmeralda told me to have fun." Lucy was relieved that May didn't say anything about her missing hand, or how it probably was hard for Lucy to wash her hair because of it. So far no one even seemed to notice her deformity, and if they did notice, it didn't seem to bother them.

May exclaimed, "Esmeralda *spoke* to you? You must really be special. You know, most people can't communicate with dragons, and most dragons wouldn't talk to us anyway. Or so I've heard."

This was news to Lucy. "Well, I've always been good with animals. I can sort of...feel what they're feeling. My father says it's all hogwash, but last week I let him know that one of our cows, Blue Moon, had a blocked teat, because Blue Moon let me know. He didn't believe me of course, but sure enough Dr. Penelope, our vet, confirmed what I'd said. But maybe my ability to communicate with cows and dogs and cats and so on—maybe it helps me hear dragons." Suddenly she shut her mouth. Had she been talking too much? No one ever wanted to talk to her.

May, however, seemed fascinated. While Lucy had been rattling on about Blue Moon, May had started to shampoo her hair. Lucy realized she'd never felt anything so soft and calming.

"That feels wonderful," Lucy said. "How long have you worked at the palace?"

May thought for a moment. "Well, officially only a year, since I turned fourteen and finished school, but my whole family lives in the palace. My mother is the cook. Just wait until you taste her food! There's no one better! I'm actually training to be a cook as well, but Clotilda thought you might prefer to have someone closer to your age to help you instead of someone older.

I started out working as a maid while I was still in school. Let's see...My father is the head gardener, and my three older brothers..." Her eyes rolled as she said that. "...work for him. I also have a younger sister who's training as a maid, as I did at first. We all live in a little cottage on the palace grounds."

Lucy was quiet as she enjoyed the soak. When it was time for her to get out, May wrapped her in a big purple towel. Lucy had understandably always had trouble getting dry after a swim in the creek, but usually it was warm enough for her to air-dry. She'd never thought of the logistics of trying to get dry after a bath. Once again, though, May kept helping without seeming to, chattering all the time. "So what's your family like? Where do you live?"

Lucy paused before she began. "We live in Cliffside on a dairy farm. It was just my mom, my dad, and me, but then there was that horrendous earthquake six years ago—"

May interrupted. "I remember hearing about that! All the dragons and their riders were sent to help and remove the injured to Havenshold, which has Draconia's best medical facilities."

"Yeah, my home was hit pretty badly. That's how I lost my right hand. My mother threw herself over me to protect me when a tree came crashing down on us and...she was killed," Lucy said quietly.

"How dreadful," said May, with a wrinkled forehead and frown. "Oh...I can't even imagine what you have been through."

"It hasn't been easy," finished Lucy, but then she smiled a little. "Um, where are my clothes?" She looked around.

May picked up instantly on the change of topic and went with it. "When we have visitors, they sometimes need new clothes, so we keep a storeroom here full of lots of stuff. Want to come scavenge with me?"

Lucy looked thunderstruck. "I couldn't take anyone else's things."

"Sure you can! That's what they're for. Come on. It'll be fun, and remember, you're supposed to have fun! Dragon's orders." May laughed. She produced a purple bathrobe for Lucy, and soon the girls headed to another room.

Closets lined the walls, and each closet was labeled with what was inside. May obviously had done this before, as she headed straight to a closet labeled, WOMEN'S UNDERGARMENTS. She pulled out a few bras and underpants for Lucy. "Let's see what fits best." Then it was on to a closet marked, TEENAGE GIRLS, and Lucy was amazed at the array of shirts and slacks. May let her choose whatever she liked, but when Lucy selected all neutrals, May suggested a pair of purple slacks and a magenta shirt.

Lucy said, "Oh, that's too bright. Everyone would see me."

May laughed. "That's the *point!* These will look super when you're riding atop Esmeralda."

Lucy shyly accepted the clothes. The minute she was dressed and then saw herself in the full-length mirror, she laughed with joy. "These are so pretty. I've never felt like this before. Are you sure this is OK?"

"Perfectly OK," said May, sounding rather proud of herself. She found some blue boots and a rich purple coat for Lucy.

It was all a little overwhelming, but Lucy felt like a new person.

As soon as Lucy was dressed, May took her to Clotilda's private office. They walked into the room, and both Clotilda and Emily looked up.

"You look fantastic!" Emily said.

Clotilda looked at May and gave her a thumbs-up that Lucy couldn't see.

"Is it OK? It isn't too much? May said it was fine. I tried to get plainer clothes, but May wouldn't have it." Lucy smiled shyly, her cheeks as bright as her shirt.

Clotilda said, "May was exactly right. You look beautiful. Personally I don't think one can have too much color." Clotilda was dressed in a bright-blue shirt with purple slacks, and Emily was all in purple.

"While you two were playing in the bathroom," Clotilda continued with a smile, "Emily and I concluded our business. May, you may tell your mother we are definitely ready for one of her fabulous lunches. Let's keep it simple and just have it served in here."

May nodded, told Lucy how happy she was to have met her, gave her a quick hug, and left.

Within a few minutes, Lucy, Emily, and Clotilda were seated around a round table that was laden with more food than Lucy and her father ate in a month. "Don't worry," said Clotilda, as she saw Lucy's eyes widen at the spread. "May's mom always sends too much, but it never goes to waste. May comes from a large family."

Lucy smiled. "She told me."

The room was silent as everyone served themselves and ate. There were mashed potatoes and baked squash, along with a wide assortment of other veggies Lucy had never seen. There were several different kinds of salads, some with greens, some with fruit. And the fruit pies looked amazing. Lucy was hesitant at first, but as she saw Emily and Clotilda filling their plates, she got bolder. Soon everyone was sitting back after a delicious meal that didn't leave many leftovers after all.

Clotilda said, "Lucy, Emily has shared with me a bit of what your last six years have been like, and I must apologize for not stepping in sooner. Red flags should have gone up for us when your father refused our medical care and took you out of the hospital hours after your surgery. Unfortunately there was so much chaos then that we slipped up."

"My father is a hard man to cross," Lucy said with a nod.

"Emily also said that she tried coming by a few times. I believe you were still in bed recovering. He seems to be violently against riders and dragons."

Lucy said, "I've never known why. He hates being dependent on anyone and barely let the visiting nurse in. He probably wouldn't have if he hadn't had a broken leg, but we managed."

"Well, if it's any comfort," continued Clotilda, "you have alerted us to a major hole in our social services in Draconia. Once you are properly situated at Havenshold and have adjusted, I'd like to meet with you again to discuss the issues of bullying and abuse that you have made us aware of. We need your help with this."

Lucy's eyes widened, and her jaw dropped. "You want me to help?"

"Definitely," affirmed Clotilda. "I understand from Emily that you have two more stops on your journey. You need to leave your school officially and quit your job."

Lucy appeared crestfallen and stared at the floor. "I guess," she muttered.

Clotilda looked at Lucy with kind gentle eyes that crinkled at the corner "I know this will be very hard, but please do your best to speak *your* truth. After all you're headed to Havenshold, but your other classmates and your coworkers are still going to be in bad situations. Anything you say could save someone else."

Lucy looked up at Clotilda and said in a small voice, "I'll try."

A little while later, Emily and Lucy headed back out to Esmeralda and took to the skies.

— 7 —

LEAVING CLIFFSIDE

Lucy couldn't believe how wonderful it was to fly. For most of the journey, she just enjoyed watching the countryside below, seeing the sheep and the cows and noticing how small they looked. They flew over a couple of small villages that looked, at least from the air, much like her own Cliffside. *But was Cliffside ever my own?* she wondered.

All too soon they were flying over Cliffside. Emily and Esmeralda landed smoothly in the schoolyard. Lucy realized that school was still in session, and she became even more nervous. Emily gave her a reassuring hug and helped her off Esmeralda. They quickly entered the one-room schoolhouse. Emily carried Lucy's backpack with the cut straps.

Mr. Jones stopped teaching and said, "Lucy, who is this? And why are you coming in just now? You're very late."

Lucy hesitated for a few minutes, clenching and unclenching her left hand as her knees shook, but then she walked to the front of the classroom, turned to Mr. Jones, and announced in a shaky voice, "I'm leaving Cliffside."

A murmur of questions ran around the room.

"Before I leave there are a few things you should know." Lucy paused. *Can I really do this?* She took a big breath and stared back at Emily, who gave her a small smile and a nod.

"Mr. Jones, yesterday I told you I spilled the honey in my desk. Well, that wasn't true." Lucy stopped for a moment, but then she stood up taller and straighter, looked Mr. Jones straight in the eye, and went on more firmly. "The honey was just another incident in a long series of bullying by Sam and his friends in the back of the room."

Sam started to protest and laugh, but Lucy continued right over his comments, speaking loudly and very swiftly. "In addition they cut the straps on my backpack, knowing it would make it difficult for anyone to carry, but especially for me. I don't know what I've done to make them bully me. Maybe it's just because I'm different, but no one has stood up for me either."

With this Lucy looked out at the students of assorted ages. Some of the older girls were ashamed enough to look down, unable to meet her glance. Lucy turned back to Mr. Jones. "Yesterday you said I'd have to pay for all of my books," she continued. "Well, I'm returning them. I won't need any of them in my new school at Havenshold."

Gasps of astonishment and lots of whispering answered this statement. As for Mr. Jones, he merely looked dumbstruck.

Lucy concluded, "You've never noticed what's going on, Mr. Jones. That group of boys, led by Sam, bullies a lot of the younger students. I wanted to bring it out into the open." Turning to the students, she finished by saying, "You don't have to be bullied. Every school and every community should have *zero* tolerance for such behavior. I stand before you now to say that if any of you is being harassed the way I was, let your parents know. If no one does anything, send word to me at Havenshold. I'll make sure you're helped." Lucy held her head high as she made her way toward the door.

Emily dropped the damaged backpack full of books on Mr. Jones's desk and followed Lucy out. She noticed a number of girls about Lucy's age staring in amazement at Lucy because of her transformed appearance with the new clothes, but more important, her transformed confidence. Emily vowed to keep an eye on the situation in Cliffside, but she thought Lucy had done a world of good for the other students with her speech.

As soon as they were outside, Lucy staggered, and Emily put an arm around her. Lucy was shaking all over.

Emily said, "I know that was incredibly difficult, but you did a fabulous job! I was ready to step in and say something, but I didn't have to. You said it all eloquently and effectively. You were very brave."

Lucy looked at Emily. "I don't know if I could have done it without you and Esmeralda with me."

Esmeralda said, *You aren't alone anymore.*

Lucy nodded and said, "This is all so new, . . .but so wonderful" she added quickly.

"OK, how to we get to the animal clinic?" Emily said.

"It's just a few blocks west of here on the outskirts of town," Lucy said.

"We'll fly anyway. I want those students to see you on Esmeralda. Besides, you two look so good together with your new clothes!"

Of course it was silly to fly, but Lucy felt very pleased with the suggestion. All the students had rushed to the windows to see her mount the dragon and to see them take off. Esmeralda took a few extra turns around the village just to be sure everyone in town saw them. She then landed easily in front of the clinic.

As soon as Lucy and Emily entered the clinic, Marta came running up to her. "Oh, Lucy! I've been so worried since you ran out of here yesterday. I tried to find you and even stopped at your farm, but no one knew where you were. Your father was very angry. Are you all right?"

Lucy gave Marta a big hug. "I was far from all right yesterday, but now my world has flipped into an incredible state. This is my friend, Emily, and that's her lovely dragon, Esmeralda, out front." Lucy felt shy about calling Emily her friend, but Emily moved forward to shake Marta's hand.

"From what Lucy has told me," Emily began, "you've been her only friend to date. Thank you for everything you've done for her."

Marta blushed. "I tried, but things here aren't very supportive. Since Lucy's the youngest one at the clinic, she's the easiest target."

Emily said, "I'd like to have everyone here gather together. Lucy has something she wants to say."

Marta looked nervous. "The staff is on break in the employee room. They don't like being interrupted."

"Show us the way. This won't take long," Emily said in a commanding tone.

As soon as they entered the staff room, there was an uproar. "Where have you been, Lucy? How dare you flounce out of here yesterday and leave us shorthanded!" roared Dr. Penelope. "Who's this?" she added with a flick of her hand toward Emily.

Everyone was staring at Lucy. They'd never seen her in decent clothes before. She stood up as tall as she could and said, "Yesterday was the last straw. You have a lovely clinic, and most of the people working here are super. They know their jobs, and they work hard. But I have to tell you, Dr. Penelope, as good as you are as a vet, you are a dreadful manager, and you have no people skills."

Gasps flew around the room. No one talked to Dr. Penelope like that! Dr. Penelope started to say something, but Lucy kept going. *If I don't say something now, I never will, and they've got to know,* she thought. She looked straight at Dr. Penelope and said, "You have no idea what's going on. Agnes bullies everyone and makes them take the blame for *her* mistakes. That's what happened yesterday. I only gave out the prescription Agnes handed me, but for some reason, you have blinders on where Agnes is concerned. Furthermore Agnes works hand in glove with Laura, who's very bitter about being demoted. They can only get away with this behavior because they see *your* bullying whenever you have a bad day. You have a position of power, and you abuse that power if someone doesn't jump fast enough for you. Why do you think you have such a high turnover rate here?"

Lucy stopped to catch her breath. There was dead silence. She finished by saying, "You're the best vet in the world, and I really admire your skills, but you need a good office manager who'll treat *everyone* fairly."

Dr. Penelope had been turning redder and redder. "How dare you speak to me like that? You deserted your post yesterday and left us dreadfully understaffed. I gave you this job because I felt sorry for you." She wasn't going to back down or apologize for anything.

Lucy blanched but continued, "I dare because I'm quitting. I wanted to say my piece for the sake of all the wonderful people here who suffer every day as I did but won't speak up for fear of losing their jobs. Please, try to understand that working in an environment where bullying is encouraged is unhealthy for everyone."

"You can't quit," Dr. Penelope said. "Your father depends on you for your salary, and certainly no one else would hire you."

Emily, seeing Lucy's eyes dropped and her hands tremble, stepped forward. "Excuse me, but Lucy already has a position. I don't think any of you ever realized Lucy's ability to communicate with animals. She told me she never mentioned it, because her father ridiculed her every time she told him. But she is *amazing*. I believe you just unblocked Blue Moon's teat. Did you know that Blue Moon was able to communicate her pain to Lucy, and that's why you were called out to the dairy farm?"

Dr. Penelope raised her eyebrows. "Really? I had no idea Lucy had that ability. I only know that surgeries go much more easily when she holds the animal."

Agnes gave a derisive snort. Emily ignored her and said to Dr. Penelope, "Then why did you never *talk* to her? She's been living for six years in an abusive situation at home, school, *and* work. She's done her very best to carry on without any support, except the comfort Marta has offered. Why didn't you notice?" Emily looked at everyone in the room then refocused her gaze on Dr. Penelope. "My dragon and I heard Lucy's pleas last night when we flew over the cave she was hiding in. Thanks to you and your terribly wrong and abusive outburst yesterday, piled on top of a day of such abuses, Lucy felt she had nowhere to go. Thankfully Esmeralda and I were in the right place at the right time. Lucy is moving into a better space. I've offered her an apprenticeship at Havenshold in our animal clinic until she finishes school. She can then work as an apprentice volcanologist, if she wishes. I paid her father to allow her to come with me. She will no longer be his slave laborer. She will go to school in Havenshold, where we have zero tolerance for bullies. She won't come to school to find her desk filled with honey or have the straps on her backpack slashed. She'll work with our Sylvester, who'll be overjoyed to have such an empathic person to help him tend to our animals. Lucy's life from here on out will be safe and fulfilling. The only question for you, Dr. Penelope, is whether you're going to learn from this and get help for you and your staff. I'll personally be back periodically to check on the situation here."

Emily placed her hand on Lucy's shoulder and turned her toward the door. No one said a thing until they were nearly out of the clinic. Marta came running up, gave Lucy another hug, and said, "I'll miss you so much! Please let me know how you're doing now and again."

Lucy hugged her back. "Of course. And thank you, Marta. You're the best."

Esmeralda was waiting for them outside. She had nearly lain flat on the street. She said to Lucy, *Hey, just grab anywhere, and see if you can get up on your own in front of these jerks.*

Lucy laughed, but she decided that climbing Esmeralda would be fun. As soon as she was on Esmeralda's back, Esmeralda stood, and Emily vaulted into her seat behind Lucy. *Well, that was sure a show! Let them talk about that! Are you having fun now, Lucy?*

Lucy smiled a big smile and waved to Marta as she said, "I sure am. Thanks, Esmeralda!"

— 8 —

ARRIVAL AT HAVENSHOLD

Lucy was exhausted. She couldn't even begin to organize her thoughts. She rested against Emily as they flew off to Havenshold. Despite everything that had just happened, she was scared that the folks at Havenshold wouldn't like her any better than most of the folks at Cliffside. What if she had just stepped out of the frying pan and into the fire?

Just as her worries were starting to spiral out of control, Emily spoke to her to help calm her. "Lucy, you were very brave back there. I know it was really hard to speak up, but you did a super job. In fact I know a lot of adults who wouldn't have been able to handle themselves so well."

Lucy murmured, "Thanks."

"But you have a right to be worried. I've yanked you out of the only world you've known, and you must be wondering what you've gotten yourself into. I can only say that we—Esmeralda and I—never will let anyone hurt you again. You also have Clotilda and Matilda in your court."

Lucy began to relax a bit. She listened as Emily went on. "I've contacted the head of the Dragon Riders, my brother Hans, and he's supported every decision I've made. He'll be waiting to meet you when we land. You can trust him as well. Now just close your eyes and relax."

"I can't close my eyes," Lucy said. "I might miss something." But she did relax and once again started to look around. They were flying over a big ranch with lots of sheep. "That's the biggest ranch I've ever seen," she exclaimed.

Emily laughed. "That's the Geldsmith ranch, owned by Baron Geldsmith."

"The guy who started a war?" Lucy asked.

"Yes," answered Emily. "But once his sons, Lance and Gregory, got him sorted out, we found out he's a pretty good guy. He bonded, at the age of *forty-three,* with a gryphon named Oswald! Now he spends most of his time in Forbury. His younger son, Lance, runs his lands now. His older son, Gregory—who happens to be my boyfriend—works as a volcanologist."

"Wow," Lucy said. She looked ahead and saw the volcano. "Are we going *in* that?"

"No, don't worry," replied Emily. "Havenshold surrounds the volcano top, and we've dug into the cliffs and rocks to make caves to live in, but we don't go inside! You can see our sheep grazing on the small amount of pasture we have. And over there, to the right—that's where the riders have their hot springs. The volcano has really helped us a lot—the riders, all of Draconia, and the other three nations as well. We all benefit from its power. We're coming up to the central courtyard of Havenshold. Everything else leads off this one spot. Oh, look! Hans is waiting for us."

Esmeralda landed in the center of the courtyard. Hans, a tall willowy man with brown hair and eyes and an enormous smile who exuded an air of calm command, came over before Emily could get Lucy down. He gave his sister a hug, and once Lucy had her feet on the ground, he said, "You must be Lucy. I've heard so much about you. Welcome to Havenshold."

Lucy shook his hand, pleased that he had offered his left hand rather than his right, and muttered, "Thank you for having me."

Hans said, "Come on into my office. I'm having dinner sent up. I gather you haven't eaten since Clotilda gave you lunch. Was it a magnificent spread as always?"

Emily laughed. "Irene is a fabulous cook. You know that."

Lucy asked, "That's May's mom, right?" before she wondered whether she should be quiet.

Hans laughed. "Right! Isn't May kind?"

Feeling more confident, Lucy said, "Oh, she was wonderful. She shampooed my hair and found me these clothes and insisted I wear *color,* and she talked all the time about her family and the palace. I couldn't keep up with it all, but it was fun." Lucy suddenly looked worried. "That was OK, wasn't it? Esmeralda told me to have fun."

Emily looked over Lucy's head at her brother to be sure he had picked up on Lucy's fear, but Hans was ahead of her. "Better than OK. Esmeralda is right. You *do* need to have fun. You can hear Esmeralda in your mind?"

"Yes," answered Lucy. "She's so much better than communicating with a cow or a dog."

Lucy heard Esmeralda snort in her head. *Did you just compare me to a cow or a dog?* But before Lucy could feel that she had goofed, Esmeralda gave a deep chuckle.

Hans and Emily were smiling as well. Hans went on, "Emily told me you were sensitive to animals. That's a rare and beautiful gift."

"My father ridiculed me for it. He said I was making it all up," answered Lucy.

"Well, he was wrong. I can't wait for you to meet Sylvester. He takes care of all our animals and runs our clinic," Hans said.

"But not today," Emily said. "Let's eat, and then I want to take you to see Beatrice, our nurse. After that..." Emily stopped long enough to look at Hans and receive his confirmation. "...I'm going to take you to my parents' home, where you'll be staying."

Lucy's jaw dropped. "I figured I'd just be in a dormitory. Are you sure your parents want me?"

Emily smiled and said, "Oh, yes. Hans, Jake, and I have all moved out permanently, and my next younger brothers, Robert and Michael, are gone most of the time. Robert is apprenticed to an architect and Michael to a botanist. Finally there's Hannah, who's now a Dragon Rider apprentice. She was selected at the last hatching three years ago by a gorgeous orange dragon named Firebolt, who was sired by Hans's Fire Dancer—keeping it all in the family, I guess." Emily chuckled. "My mother keeps complaining about the empty house and how she and my father rattle around in it. She jumped at the chance to have another child to foster, as did my father. Now they have someone new to tell all their stories to about their dragon-riding days."

"Your parents were Dragon Riders too?" Lucy asked.

"They retired from active duty when I was born," Hans said, "but they like nothing more than to go out flying. They used to give us rides all the time."

That settled it for Lucy. Maybe she could get rides sometimes too. Just then the food was brought in. It was plain, simple fare—meat, potatoes, and vegetables—but there was plenty of it, and it was hot and tasty.

After dinner Emily and Lucy left for the hospital, where Lucy was scheduled to meet with Nurse Beatrice. Lucy started to get nervous again. She didn't like anyone looking at her arm or her angry red scar, but Emily was adamant.

Lucy was pleasantly surprised by Nurse Beatrice. She was a middle-aged woman with salt-and-pepper hair, a no-nonsense look about her, and a kind smile. Beatrice motioned Lucy into the examining room and told Emily to come back in a half-hour. Emily gave Lucy a smile and said she would be back.

Beatrice checked Lucy's blood pressure, pulse and temperature, all the time talking about how happy they were to have found her. "I was so worried after the earthquake when your father took the two of you out of here an *hour* after your surgery. I've thought of you often, but I should have followed up on those thoughts. The visiting nurse reported that she'd seen you a couple times to be sure you were getting your medicine and to change the bandage, but then your father refused any more visits. He doesn't like Havenshold."

"It's OK," Lucy said. "I did all right. I don't want to cause any trouble."

"Trouble?" Beatrice said, as she jotted notes in the chart she had set up for Lucy. "You've done us all a huge favor. I haven't seen Havenshold so shaken up in a long time. We thought things were going well for all of Draconia, and then we find out about you and that mess in Cliffside. The main thing Dragon Riders do for Draconia is make sure that *everyone* is living the best lives they can. We pride ourselves on our caring, on our looking after folks. Here in Havenshold everyone looks after everyone else. We have our folks who don't like other folks, just like anywhere. The difference here is that we all know we have to rely on each other, so likes and dislikes don't matter. Helping each other is the way we work."

"I like that," Lucy said with a smile, thinking it sounded too good to be true.

"And we were foolish enough to think that was true in all the villages and towns of Draconia. You've given us a rude awakening!" proclaimed Beatrice, closing the chart and standing up.

"I'm sorry," Lucy said, dropping her gaze and folding her arms around her as she sat in the examining chair.

"No 'sorry' about it. You did a wonderful thing, and you can be sure that some very positive changes will take place because of your bravery. But enough of that. Let's see that arm of yours."

Lucy reluctantly held out her right arm. Beatrice looked and made *tut, tut, tut* noises. The scar, even after all these years, was still a large, raised, angry red welt, and Lucy flinched when Beatrice poked it gently. She said, "Obviously you had no further treatments, and I assume no physical therapy. How are you managing? Emily says you were doing all the cooking and cleaning, mucking out stables and feeding cows, and even working at an animal clinic, so my guess is you've figured out a lot."

"I did what I had to," Lucy said, jutting out her chin defiantly.

"Well, you've done really well," answered Beatrice. "I'd like to show you some things, though, that might make your life a bit easier. You don't have to, but you should at least know what's available. OK? Come with me."

Beatrice took Lucy to a room filled with crutches, wheelchairs, canes, walkers, and all sorts of drawers filled with things she didn't even recognize. "Dragon Riders get injured often, so we've had to come up with a lot of equipment to help those whose injuries—like yours—are permanent. Let me show you some things that might help you."

Beatrice opened a drawer. There were leather cups with straps, hooks, and clamps. Lucy started to back away, but Beatrice blocked her. "You don't have to use any of these if you don't want, but I do intend to let you know what's *possible*. Obviously we can't give you your hand back, but these straps and cups can be made to fit comfortably over your stump, and you can add various attachments as needed. Carrying things is much easier with a hook, for instance, and one of our riders managed to fashion this clamp so she could clip a comb into it to comb her hair." Beatrice glanced over at Lucy to see how she was taking in all of this, and she was startled to see tears pouring down Lucy's cheeks. "Oh, honey," she said, sweeping Lucy into her ample breast. "I didn't mean to upset you."

Lucy said, "I'm sorry. It's just that...I used to have long hair, like Emily's, and my mother combed and braided it for me every morning. It was our special time. After the earthquake, I had to cut off my hair because I couldn't manage it myself."

Beatrice kindly said, "I wondered about your hair... It is rather jagged."

"My father would never pay to have anyone cut it. He told me I could do it myself and it didn't matter what it looked like," Lucy sobbed.

"Well, don't you worry now. I hear you're staying with the Morrises. Amy Morris, Emily's mom, is a dab hand at hair. I know she'd be thrilled to help you out. Your life has turned a corner, and only good lies ahead. Maybe later on you'll want to grow your hair out, knowing that you'll be able to comb it yourself once we get your scar taken care of. Then, if you want, you can be fitted with a cup for the stump which you can then add a hook or a variety of clamps to. But only if you want."

Lucy dried her eyes. "Thanks," she said. "Everyone is being so kind to me."

"And why shouldn't we be?" answered Beatrice. "Now about your arm—I want you to come back in the morning and have our doctor look at it. I'm not sure, but I think he can do something about that scar to make it less painful. You can't be fitted for any helping tools until you've properly healed. You'll get some physical therapy, but the doctor will be able to tell you more. We have one of the best surgeons in the world, Dr. Brian. Just wait and see."

Beatrice took Lucy to the reception area, where Emily was waiting.

"All set?" Emily asked as Lucy walked toward her.

Beatrice nodded. "Lucy is underfed and a bit malnourished—which isn't surprising—but your mom will fix that. I'm concerned about her scar, so I want her back here tomorrow morning around ten to see Dr. Brian. Otherwise she's good to go!"

Emily looked at Lucy, who gave her a weak smile. "I talked with my mom and told her you were to have my old room. I think you'll be happiest there. The guest room is OK but a bit cold. I think your quilt will look *super* on my old bed. Let's get you home. You look about ready to drop! You've had so much happen, and you've done so much in less than twenty-four hours."

Lucy nodded, her eyes drooping sleepily, and turning to Nurse Beatrice said, "Thank you. I'll be here tomorrow." She staggered a bit from exhaustion as she started to leave, but Emily was at her side.

Emily put an arm around Lucy, and they headed out the door.

— 9 —

A NEW HOME

Emily steered Lucy to the central courtyard, where Esmeralda stood waiting. "I thought tonight, as it's been such a long day, we'd have Esmeralda fly us home. It's not a long walk, but I think any walk is too much for you right now. You don't mind, do you?" Emily asked with a smile.

"Mind?" Lucy said. Suddenly she felt more awake. "I love riding Esmeralda—anytime, anywhere."

"Great!" Soon they were in the air, and nearly as soon, Esmeralda had landed in a large field behind a rambling house. A tall, thin, gray-haired lady hurried over to them.

"Emily!" said the woman, whom Lucy realized must be Emily's mom, Amy. They hugged, and then Emily introduced Lucy.

"I'm so thrilled that you'll be staying with us. The house seems so empty now. A foster daughter is just the blessing we need," Amy said.

Lucy looked a bit overwhelmed. *Foster parents?* She didn't quite understand.

Emily placed her hand on Lucy's shoulder. "When we take someone as an apprentice here at Havenshold, we always make sure they have a foster family to live with—people who will care about them and treat them as their own. When your father relinquished his guardianship of you to us, it was with that proviso."

Lucy answered thoughtfully, "I suspect he would have signed anything for the money, but I'm thankful for your care, Emily. Amy, I'm very excited to have you and your husband as foster parents. I'll work hard for you. I promise."

Emily and her mom exchanged glances, but neither said anything. Instead Amy responded, "Come on in, and I'll show you around."

Emily said, "I have to get back, but I'll be here in the morning. Lucy has an appointment with Dr. Brian at ten. Lucy, you're in good hands here—safe and friendly—so just enjoy settling in, and get a good night's sleep. See you both tomorrow!"

With a quick hug for each of them, Emily raced over to Esmeralda. Before Lucy could blink, they were gone. Lucy started to panic, but immediately Amy put an arm around her and said, "Let me show you where you'll sleep. We'll wait until morning for the grand tour. You've had enough for today. Emily insisted that you have her room. I don't know why no one ever wants to use our guest room."

Lucy was glad that Amy kept up a constant patter, just as May had done in the palace. It made it easier for Lucy to look around and adjust. They walked through the back door into a large and inviting kitchen. Amy said, "With a family as big as ours, this room is the center of the house. Someone is *always* eating or cooking."

They walked down a long hall with a lot of open doors that led to bedrooms, each in a different color and a different state of tidiness. "The house grew rather randomly with each new baby, with bits and pieces stuck anywhere. Started out as a two-bedroom, and now it's an eight-bedroom with *four* bathrooms. Good thing Todd's handy," Amy teased. "You'll meet him tomorrow. He's out at a meeting now, but he wanted me to tell you how pleased he is to have you here too."

The hall seemed to go on forever, twisting and turning, but finally Amy led Lucy into a purple bedroom. "Emily *had* to have a purple bedroom even before she bonded with Esmeralda. Some things are just meant to be, I guess. Anyway, let's get your things unpacked." She lifted Lucy's quilt out of her hands.

They spread everything out on the bed, and Lucy suddenly felt ashamed. It looked like such a small bundle. The clothes were threadbare and worn, but Amy didn't give Lucy any time to think. "Let's put your things in this drawer and then spread the quilt over the bed. It's such a lovely quilt," remarked Amy.

"My mother made it for my sixth birthday," Lucy said. She was proud of the quilt. It was the nicest and most precious thing she owned.

"I can see she was very talented," Amy said. "I sure never made anything this lovely. Do you have pajamas?"

Lucy turned red and muttered, "I usually just sleep in my underwear and an old shirt."

Amy laughed. "I know all about that! Easy, comfy, and fast. Let's see if any of Emily's pajamas might still be here and might fit. She's a bit taller than you and a bit heavier, but still..." Amy rummaged through some other drawers and found something to her liking. "Here you go. The bathroom is through that door." She pointed to a door on the far side of the room. "You get into these and scoot into bed. I'll go make you a mug of hot choco-late."

"Oh, you don't have to go to any trouble," stammered Lucy, unused to attention like this and feeling very uncomfortable.

"Don't be silly. It's no trouble at all. I always did that for my kids. It's just a pleasant way to end the day." She left the room with a smile.

Lucy went into the bathroom, which she was glad to see wasn't fancy, just clean and functional. All the towels were purple, and she was happy about that. They made her feel like Emily and Esmeralda were there with her. She got ready for bed quickly then slid under the covers, feeling her quilt with her fingertips, and noticing that Amy had tucked all Lucy's stuffed animals under the covers, including her old soft teddy bear who was poking out from under her pillow. Lucy held onto her bear as she looked around the room. All the walls were lined with shelves. There was another door, which Lucy thought probably led to a closet, and there were a couple dressers under some of the shelves. The shelves were filled with an assortment of books and stuffed animals. A large stuffed dragon sat prominently in the middle of the wall across from the bed. Lucy felt it would be a good guardian.

Amy came in with the promised mug of hot chocolate. She sat on the bed as Lucy drank it. "Well, you've had a long day full of new adventures—some wonderful and I'd imagine some not so wonderful—but you're safe here now, and we're going to look after you, just the way we looked after our other six."

Lucy thought it sounded wonderful to be included like that. "Thank you so much. You've been so kind to me."

"Now you just snuggle under the covers and get a good night's sleep. Todd and I have a room three doors down the hallway if you need anything," she said, as she took Lucy's mug. She surprised Lucy by giving her a kiss on the top of her head.

Lucy was asleep almost before she got comfy. Amy looked satisfied. She'd slipped a mild sleeping medication into the hot chocolate after Emily had explained about Lucy's nightmares. *Tonight,* Amy determined, *Lucy will have a good night's sleep.* Amy turned and left the room, quietly shutting the door.

The next morning Lucy woke up to sun streaming through the bedroom window and across the bed. For a minute she was scared. She was supposed to be mucking out the barn and doing all her chores. But then she remembered that she was in Emily's room, safe at Havenshold. She got out of bed and wondered what she should be doing. As soon as she started to move around the room, she heard a knock at the door. She called, "Come in," and a very tall man with gray hair, startling blue eyes, and the biggest smile she'd ever seen walked in.

"Hi. I'm Todd, Emily's dad. Sorry I missed meeting you last night. We're so happy to have you here." He held a piece of toast in his hand, and he waved it around as he talked.

"Thank you for having me," Lucy said, her eyes downcast.

"The more, the merrier. That's what I always say. I'm headed out for the day, but Amy asked me to show you the way to the kitchen. She has breakfast all ready for you. So if you're set, let's navigate the twists and turns of this old house."

Lucy smiled. Emily's dad was funny—nothing like her dad. For just a moment, she felt sad, but Todd was jogging down the hallway, so she followed suit. By the time they got to the kitchen, both of them were laughing.

Amy, smiling, looked up from the stove. "I see you've met the comedian of the family! Have a seat, and I'll dish up some breakfast."

Todd went over and gave Amy a big hug and a kiss. "See you ladies tonight." He headed out the door with a wave.

Amy had made scrambled eggs and sausage, which she set down in front of Lucy. "Hope you like this."

The look in Lucy's eyes was enough for Amy. It was obvious that Lucy didn't have breakfasts like this and that no one had been cooking for her.

"It's wonderful," Lucy said, "but I should have made yours."

"Not in this house, you don't. We'll do some cooking together later, for fun, but this is my domain. I take pride and pleasure in feeding my family. Don't you worry. You'll have enough to be getting on with once you start school and your apprenticeship."

"When will that be?" Lucy asked, surprised when her voice shook a little with apprehension.

"Not for a week. I talked with Emily and Hans, and I said I needed a week with you to help you settle in. You need time to adjust to all the new things in your life, so we're going to take it very slowly. You'll be having surgery on that arm, maybe even today, and you'll also need clothes and school supplies. You'll need to find your way around more than just this rambling old house, and I want to be able to introduce you to our friends."

Lucy felt scared, but the thought of delaying school for a week was appealing, so she just nodded and continued to eat her breakfast.

After the meal, they returned to Lucy's new bedroom. "Now let's see if we can find you something to wear," Amy said. "I still have some of Hannah's things, and she's only two years older than you, so I bet we'll find something you'll like. You'll like Hannah. She's a lot quieter than Emily but just as caring."

Lucy was dressed in blue slacks and a yellow shirt. Everyone seemed determined to get her into color. She had to admit that while it was startling to see herself dressed like this, it felt good. In fact it was a big morale booster.

Amy glanced at the kitchen clock. "We don't have time to do any shopping today, at least not before your doctor's appointment. Emily will be here any minute."

As she said that, Emily walked through the door. "Hey, don't you look smart!" she said to Lucy as she kissed her mother. "All set?"

Lucy nodded. She said goodbye to Amy, and they headed out the door. "I thought we'd walk this morning so you could get a feel for Havenshold. Families of non-Dragon Riders—as well as families of retired Dragon Riders who are raising families, like my parents—live in these houses," Emily said, waving her hand.

"There are a lot of them," Lucy said, as she looked out at houses scattered as far as she could see.

"Yes, the Havenshold community is about three times the size of Cliffside and very diverse. The active Dragon Riders live in caves, up close and personal with the volcano. The dragons love the heat, but everyone else finds or builds a home in this general area. Most homes have large fields around them so dragons can land. My parents' home is closer to the main courtyard complex than many of the others. It makes it easy to access school, the health center, and so forth."

Lucy looked around as they walked and couldn't help notice that most of the homes seemed newer or larger than the Morrises'. Soon she spotted the courtyard ahead. "So...I have to see Dr. Brian now?" she asked.

"Yep, but you'll like him, and I think he can help you. Just listen to what he suggests, OK? No one will make you do anything you don't want."

"Can you stay with me?" Lucy asked, her voice almost a whisper.

"Of course!" answered Emily with a smile.

They walked into the health center and let the receptionist know why they were there. Soon Nurse Beatrice was bustling through a door, looking very happy to see them. "Dr. Brian is ready to see you now," she said with a kind smile, and ushered them through to an examining room.

Dr. Brian walked in. Lucy thought he was kind of cute and very young for a doctor. He had short blond hair, blue eyes, and wire-framed glasses. He also was really tall. He came over and greeted them both. "OK, let me see that arm of yours," he said, and Lucy reluctantly held it out. He felt the scar, pressing gently in several places. Lucy winced.

"That's pretty painful, isn't it? Even after..." He looked at his notes. "...six years."

"I'm used to it, mostly," answered Lucy.

"Well, I could easily make this scar a lot less noticeable, and more important, a lot less painful. You'll need to have me do that if you hope to try out any of the aids that Nurse Beatrice showed you. I could even do it this morning if you'd like."

Lucy looked at Emily with wide eyes. Emily said, "Dr. Brian has been working on Dragon Riders for many years. He's an excellent surgeon. You can trust him."

Lucy looked down at the floor. She didn't say anything for several moments. "Do I need to have this done because my father took me home too soon and wouldn't let the nurses who came to see us help me?" she asked.

Dr. Brian looked at Emily for some sort of clue as to how to answer this question, but Emily was no help at all. He said, "Sometimes these welts form anyway, but if you had stayed here, and if you had come back for some physical therapy, I think we could have helped you sooner. That isn't to say we can't fix it all right now and have you better than new, though."

Lucy nodded. She was silent for a few moments before saying, "I'd like to try. It hurts...and it would be good to have the pain go away, if you can do it. If you can't, well, at least I'll know we tried."

Emily smiled and said, "I think that's the right decision."

Dr. Brian agreed. "I'll have Nurse Beatrice come in and prep you. She'll give you a gown to wear so we that don't take any chances with that lovely outfit you have on. Emily, if you want, you can stay with her through the whole thing. It won't take more than a half-hour, tops."

Pleading with her eyes, Lucy looked up at Emily, who said, "Of course I'll stay."

The health center staff was quick and efficient. Lucy was given a gown to change into and was asked to lie on a chair that looked like a recliner. Nurse Beatrice gave her a shot to relax her, and soon she felt really dreamy. A table was fastened to the side of the chair, and Lucy's right arm was strapped down. Nurse Beatrice gave Lucy another shot—this time in her arm—so she wouldn't feel anything. Emily chatted with Lucy the entire time, telling her about what school was like in Havenshold and how super Sylvester was with animals. Lucy couldn't really focus on what Emily was saying, but her voice comforted her, and soon she closed her eyes and drifted off.

The next thing she knew, Dr. Brian was saying, "All done. It went really well. I think you'll be pleased. It's bandaged now. I'll need to see you again tomorrow to change the dressing. How are you feeling?"

Lucy opened her eyes, looked at her bandaged arm, then glanced at Emily. "It's all done?"

"Yep," Emily said. "Now we need to get you home for some of my mother's wonderful TLC. Thanks, Dr. Brian. I'll be sure she's back tomorrow morning." Emily said goodbye and helped Lucy out of the health center.

Out in front Lucy was pleased to see Esmeralda waiting to take them home.

— 10 —

THE MOLES

Later that afternoon Lucy was walking in the backyard, feeling strangely happy. She and Amy had shared a quiet lunch, and then Amy had shooed her out of the kitchen, telling her to rest. Her arm wasn't hurting, although she tried not to jostle it. Emily had mentioned that Dr. Brian had given her a shot of a twenty-four-hour pain medication, which should keep her comfortable until she saw him tomorrow, but Lucy didn't want to risk hurting it.

Lucy noticed a bench on the edge of the grassy pasture and headed there to sit and sort out everything that had happened to her in the past two days. It was too cold to stay out for long, but she was wearing the wonderful purple coat May had given her, and at the moment, she was comfortably warm.

Lucy sat and relaxed, noticing how quiet it was. Suddenly she felt her thoughts touch someone else. She couldn't see anyone, but feelings definitely were coming her way. It took her a few minutes to realize it, but what she was sensing was a community of moles living under the bench at the edge of the pasture. She'd never communicated with moles before. Lucy was excited. She reached her thoughts toward them, and she sensed happiness, contentment, and bustling activity. She sat quietly and concentrated on the mole activity. They had picked that spot because it was near a volcanic steam vent. They wouldn't go farther into the pasture, as it got too hot for them underground, but here on the edge was the perfect spot.

While the moles were warm, Lucy was getting cold, so she headed inside. As she walked into the kitchen, Amy was preparing dinner.

Amy looked up and said, "I've been thinking. Would you like me to cut your hair? I do it for all the kids—well, when they let me—and Emily mentioned you'd had to do your own. I think it's really great that you can cut your own hair, but it also must be hard."

Lucy didn't hesitate. "I'd love that. Everyone has always made fun of my hair, but my father wouldn't let anyone else cut it. But you're busy—"

"Nonsense. I'm just about done here. Have a seat at the table, and I'll find my hair scissors." A few moments later, Amy returned with scissors and a mirror in hand. She wrapped a towel around Lucy's shoulders then said, "Now how would you like it cut? Any ideas?"

Lucy remembered what Nurse Beatrice had said about maybe being able to use a comb. "I think I'd like to grow it a bit longer," answered Lucy, mentioning the comb that Beatrice had showed her. "If I can manage it, that is."

"Well, you won't know if you don't try. It's pretty uneven right now. Why don't we start by evening it up? That might mean going a bit shorter in places, but it'll look as if we meant to do it. Then, as you heal and learn what you can do, you can decide about growing it out or not. Look at Clotilda. Her hair is always short and neat, and she doesn't have to fuss with it. Time will tell what suits you best." She quickly got to work.

As they were finishing up, Todd walked into the kitchen. Amy got him a cup of coffee and some tea for Lucy then finished working on dinner.

Lucy remembered about the moles, and she thought Todd and Amy might be interested, so when there was a break in the conversation, she related her encounter. Lucy was totally unprepared for Todd's enthusiastic response.

"You know, I've always wondered why the snow is thinnest on the pasture and why it melts the fastest there. Fern and Jupiter love it out there," he said. Lucy hadn't met his green dragon, Jupiter, or Amy's green dragon, Fern. Once that was all explained, Todd took off again. "I wonder if we could tap into that and build a big sandpit for them."

Amy laughed. "See what you've started, Lucy! Calm down, Todd. Digging into a steam vent isn't like knocking a hole in a wall and putting a door in." Lucy looked puzzled, so Amy explained, "I'm sure you've noticed how our home shakes a little. Well, every time I told Todd we were expecting, he immediately knocked a hole in the nearest wall, put a door in, and built a room on. He said if I could be growing the baby, he could be growing the room. It worked out pretty well. He'd always be finishing up the final touches as I went into labor."

Lucy chuckled. "Makes sense," she said, smiling at them both.

"But Todd, honestly, volcanoes are dangerous. You'd better check with Gregory before you do anything," Amy warned. Then she turned to Lucy. "Gregory is Emily's boyfriend. He's a volcanologist."

Lucy nodded.

"Oh, I'm just going to have a look," Todd said. "Come on, Lucy. You can show me where these moles of yours are." Lucy managed to snatch her coat as he hustled her out the door.

They hadn't been in the backyard long when Lucy said, "I think some dragons are coming."

"Yeah," Todd said absently as he paced the pasture. "I asked Fern and Jupiter to come over and help me plan the size of the sandpit. Looks like Amy sent for Gregory—Esmeralda has two riders. Sometimes I think those women don't trust me," he said with a chuckle.

Lucy stepped back near the bench. She'd never seen so many dragons up close. As soon as everyone had landed, Emily came over to introduce her to those she didn't already know. Fern and Jupiter were friendly and quite lovely. Jupiter was a dark iridescent green and about eighteen feet in length. Fern was a bit smaller, maybe sixteen feet, and a lovely bright neon green. They made a lovely pair. *But not as gorgeous as Esmeralda,* Lucy thought.

Esmeralda quickly said, *Why, thank you, but don't let them know that,* and gave one of her deep laughs.

Todd made Lucy tell everyone about the moles and what she'd learned. Fern, Jupiter, and Esmeralda confirmed that this was one of the warmest pastures around Havenshold. Gregory grabbed some charts out of a holder that hung from Esmeralda's saddle and unrolled one. "You're right, Lucy—or should I say, your moles are right."

Lucy smiled then looked down at her feet. Gregory was very tall, slim, and had brown hair and eyes. She noticed that his eyes had a twinkle in them. She thought, as she watched everyone in the backyard turning toward him *He definitely has a charismatic personality.*

Before she could say anything, Gregory continued, "You know, Todd, this could be the answer to a problem we're having with the volcano. Pressure seems to be building up here and here," he said, as he pointed to a couple of places along the same steam vent. "If we tapped into the vent to release heat into a sandpit, that might be enough to calm the volcano. But

I'd have to run some figures first. Please don't start anything until I do."

Everyone, Todd included, was having a good laugh as another man walked out of the kitchen and into the yard. He looked like a younger version of Todd. Emily saw him first and ran over and gave him a big hug. "Hi, Robert. I suppose Mom called you about Dad's latest idea. Please, come meet Lucy."

Robert reached out his left hand to Lucy, which surprised her, as most people didn't even think that she wouldn't be able to shake with the right. He was more serious than the others but clearly very sensitive as the natural use of a left-handed handshake demonstrated. "Nice to meet you," he said. "I've heard wonderful things about you. Glad you're here to keep my parents in line."

"What?" spluttered Todd. "Whatever do you mean?" He smiled as he walked over to give Robert a hug.

"You just leap and hope Jupiter will catch you!" Robert said.

"Well, he always does, one way or another," said Todd.

Robert shook his head before walking over to Gregory and the maps. "What's he up to now?" Robert asked. Gregory told the whole story. Robert looked at Lucy with a respectful gleam in his eye. "You can communicate with other species?"

Lucy turned beet red, looked down at her feet, and said, "Yes, some of them. I'm not really sure how many. I've only worked with cows, sheep, and dogs before, but today I sensed the moles."

"Wow!" Robert exclaimed. "Now *that* is something." He turned back to Todd. "Dad, you have to go easy. Gregory needs to crunch his numbers, and if you'll take it, I'd like to draw up some plans for you. There has to be some advantage to having an architect in the family. How big do you want the sandpit? And where?"

Todd looked a bit flustered. "I don't know. I was just going to put something out here," he said, waving his arms wildly around.

Lucy was very surprised when Jupiter spoke out loud. She knew dragons could use human speech, but she never had heard one do so before that moment.

"It won't be just Fern and me here, if you make a proper sandpit," Jupiter said in a deep voice that seemed to resonate from the depths of his belly. "I can think of at least four others who will come in a heartbeat. Have you forgotten there are six Dragon Riders in this family, and one of them is partnered with another rider? That's seven of us!"

As he finished saying that, everyone looked up to see Fire Dancer—who was bright orange, as her name indicated—landing. Hans jumped down. Right behind them, Harmony, a lovely brown dragon, set down softly, and Emily's brother Jake hopped off just as his partner, William, came in on his own brown dragon, Thunder.

Lucy was feeling a bit overwhelmed by all the new faces, but just as she thought she might panic, she felt Amy's arm around her. Amy said, "Well, isn't this fun? I suppose you've all dropped in for dinner! This is how this house works, Lucy—total chaos. Hannah won't be here, as she's training and Firebird is still too young to fly, and Michael is off on a botanical fact-finding mission, so you'll meet him another day."

Jake, William, and Hans came over to Lucy. She was taken by how friendly they all were. Jake was just as tall as his older brother, Hans, but he had a heavier build. His brown hair and eyes, along with a giant smile, proclaimed him to be another of Amy and Todd's children. He had his arm around William's shoulder in an affectionate way and William looked just as much at home as Jake and Hans. William was also very tall, but a tow-head and very skinny. He appeared to be a few years younger than Jake. Lucy thought they made a very handsome couple. After Lucy met Jake and William, Hans took her aside for a few minutes to make sure she was doing OK. Lucy could see even in the brief contacts she'd had with him just why Hans was the leader of the dragon riders. He was a very good listener and he picked up quickly on the situations around him. He seemed to lead by example and by a very quiet assertiveness that Lucy had never experienced before but which she was most grateful for.

"Thanks, Hans," Lucy said. "It's all so wonderful. I can't believe how friendly everyone is to me."

"And why shouldn't they be?" Hans asked with mock seriousness. "You need to remember what a wonderful person you are. If you weren't, you never would have survived. Now, for a bit at least, let my mom mother you as you deserve. Later in the week, we'll talk about school and your after school apprenticeship, but for now just get comfortable being here. Havenshold is used to having young people as fosters. Your situation isn't that different from others', as you'll find out when you get to school. Meanwhile try to keep my father from going too crazy." He smiled and gave her a hug.

Amy called, "Dinner's on!"

There was a race to the table. Lucy felt pleased to be part of such a loving family. She heard Robert and Gregory trying to convince Todd to wait for the weekend before he did anything rash. Todd nodded, caught Lucy's eye, and winked.

— 11 —

SCHOOL

The rest of the week sped by. Lucy's arm was healing really well, and Dr. Brian was pleased. She didn't need a bandage by week's end. Amy had insisted on taking her to a store that sold recycled clothes. Amy told her that everyone donated clothes they no longer needed and that anyone new to Havenshold could supplement their wardrobe very reasonably. Lucy felt funny having Amy buy her clothes, but Amy insisted it was part of fostering. Amy was someone who didn't seem to accept the word "no" at all. She also gave Lucy some really pretty things that Hannah had outgrown, so by the first day of school, Lucy felt confident that her wardrobe would pass muster with anyone.

Todd was still determined to make a sandpit, but he had waited until the weekend, although he kept asking Lucy to walk him around and let him know just where the mole tunnels were. Lucy thought that was really kind of him, since the moles had started all of this. She wouldn't have wanted them to lose their homes just because she had communicated with them. By Sunday evening Gregory and Robert had helped Todd lay out the pit, and Gregory had figured out that this would help stabilize the volcano as well as keep Todd happy.

Monday morning came faster than Lucy wanted. She wore the outfit May had given her for luck, grabbed her new backpack, assured Amy that she knew the way, and headed off to school, which was located along the eastern side of the main courtyard.

As she approached the school, she was surprised to see Hans talking to a lady who looked like a teacher and was holding a clipboard. Hans introduced Lucy to Miss Raven, and said, "I'll be here after school to take you to meet Sylvester at our animal clinic. Enjoy your first day." He said goodbye and headed toward his office.

Miss Raven, an elderly lady who was nearly as short as her cropped grey hair with green eyes that sparkled in the sunshine, said, "Welcome. Come on in. We're informal here. It's just a one-room school with about twenty students aged five through fourteen, so you'll get to know everyone quickly. We have another student from Cliffside as well, so that should make it easier for you, although of course if she is accepted by a dragon in two weeks she will leave our school for her apprenticeship."

Miss Raven turned to enter the classroom, and Lucy nearly panicked. *Another Cliffside student? Who? Will they tease me? I never had a single friend in Cliffside except Marta. Who could it be?* Lucy had no choice except to follow. Miss Raven brought her to the front of the class to introduce her, and as Lucy looked out at the other students, she immediately spotted a familiar face with green eyes surrounded by long thick curly red hair, whom Lucy realized was a girl from her old school named Gretchen. Gretchen's mouth dropped open when she saw Lucy, but she quickly shut it and looked down at her desk. *Great*, thought Lucy.

Miss Raven led Lucy to an empty desk next to Gretchen's. Lucy slid into the desk and kept her eyes down also.

The morning seemed to go on for an eternity. While the other students were working, Miss Raven gave Lucy a stack of test papers to complete, so that she could evaluate what Lucy had learned previously. Lucy didn't find them difficult. She'd always enjoyed schoolwork. When lunchtime rolled around, Lucy stayed at her desk and asked Miss Raven if she could keep working, but Miss Raven said, "No, you need a break. Do you have a lunch?"

Lucy nodded. Amy had packed her a large lunch and put it in her backpack. Miss Raven went on, "Let me show you where we eat." Lucy had no choice but to follow. Soon she was in a small room with long tables. Miss Raven went over to Gretchen and asked if she would show Lucy around.

Both girls looked embarrassed, but Lucy had no choice but to sit next to Gretchen. As soon as Miss Raven walked away, Gretchen glanced at Lucy, then down at her own lunch, and muttered softly, "I'm sorry."

Lucy was so surprised that she said, "Excuse me?" She couldn't believe Gretchen was apologizing to her.

Gretchen looked at her with moistened eyes and said, "I knew Sam and the others were bullying you, and I know I should have stood up for you, but I was scared and didn't want them to start on me, so I just looked away and pretended I didn't see."

Lucy was dumbfounded. She never would have guessed that anyone would feel as if they had to stand up for her, and Gretchen was even a year younger and small for her age. Lucy said, "That's OK. They were scary. When did you come to Havenshold?"

Gretchen, relieved that Lucy had changed the subject, answered, "Two weeks ago, when I was selected as a candidate for the upcoming hatching. We have lots to learn, so any of the candidates who don't already live in Havenshold are brought here at least through the hatching. I guess if they aren't picked,

they go back home. I don't know. A really super family is fostering me. I like it here a lot. How about you?"

Lucy hesitated then decided she would just speak the truth
and see what happened. She told Gretchen about the most
horrendous day after lots of ghastly days and how Emily and
Esmeralda had rescued her.

"Oh, Lucy!" exclaimed Gretchen. "Now I feel even worse. I
knew you had to work, but I had no idea how bad things were.
I thought it was just the school bullies—not that that wasn't a
lot. How sad!"

"Well, it's good now," Lucy said. "Emily has gotten me an
apprenticeship in Havenshold's animal clinic. I start today. And
I'm being fostered as well—by Emily's family—and they're terrific. I wish like *anything* that I'd been chosen as a candidate,
because I want to be a Dragon Rider more than anything. Riding dragons is fantastic, but with this..." She indicated her missing hand. "...I'd never be picked. Even so, I'm here, and that's
wonderful."

"You've ridden on a dragon!" exclaimed Gretchen. "What
was it like?"

The girls talked happily through the lunch hour. Miss Raven,
watching through the door, smiled.

The afternoon zoomed by. Lucy finished all her tests before
the end of the school day, and Miss Raven promised she would
have placed her in the correct levels of all her subjects by the
next day. Lucy and Gretchen headed out the door together,
and Lucy spotted Hans. The two girls went over to him, and
Lucy introduced Gretchen.

"I figured you two probably knew each other," Hans said.
"You're being fostered by Emily's friend Anne's family, aren't
you, Gretchen?"

Gretchen nodded. "They're wonderful."

"Good," Hans said. "Well, I need to show Lucy where the animal clinic is. I think you probably have candidate duties."

"Yes," Gretchen told Hans. "See you tomorrow, Lucy. I'm so glad you're here."

"Thanks," Lucy said then turned to follow Hans.

They walked around the courtyard, past the medical clinic, and turned a corner. Then Lucy saw another building surrounded by several barns.

"Sylvester is very eager to meet you," Hans said. "Your fame precedes you. Sylvester and Gregory are good friends, and Gregory couldn't wait to tell him about your moles."

Lucy turned red and looked at her feet. "Oh," she said in a small voice.

"Sylvester has a real gift with animals. He's helped me nurse Fire Dancer on several occasions, and he's one of the few non-riders who can speak telepathically with dragons. I think you both will get on really well."

They arrived at the front door of the clinic, and Hans escorted her in. The receptionist looked up and said, "I'll find Sylvester for you."

After a couple of minutes, Sylvester came through the far doorway and greeted Hans. "Great to see you, Hans. Is this my new apprentice?"

"Yes," answered Hans. "I was just telling her that I think you two will make a great team."

Sylvester looked at Lucy. He was of medium height and had long, light-brown hair tied back in a ponytail, green eyes, and a dimple in one cheek when he smiled. "So you understand moles, I hear?" he began, and Lucy turned bright red. "And now Todd is making an enormous sandpit to make the dragons happy and also relieve pressure on the volcano. Not bad for your first week here." He laughed in a happy way.

"I'll leave you to it. Don't let him work you too hard, Lucy. Remember, he can only keep you for two hours on school days and then all day Saturday with Sundays off. See you later," Hans said, as he headed out of the clinic.

Sylvester turned to Lucy. "I know you haven't been in Havenshold long, and today was your first day at school, so I won't do much today except show you around and get to know you. Ask any questions you want. I'm a very informal, easygoing guy."

Sylvester began to explain the layout of the clinic. He introduced her to Rose, their receptionist, and showed her the operating room, recovery room, and examining rooms. "In this building we take care of small animals like dogs, cats, rabbits, and I suppose even moles if we get them." He gave her a sly look. "Larger animals—horses, cows, sheep, and dragons—stay outside. We don't have many horses, as most horses can't tolerate being around dragons, but there are a few." As they walked out of the building and to the barns, Sylvester continued, "We raise cows and sheep primarily for meat and dairy for us and the dragons. Havenshold is completely self-sufficient. We need to be so that we can be independent and impartial."

"Makes sense," Lucy said. "Does that cow over there have a bad hoof?"

Sylvester looked at her with wide eyes. "Yes. How did you know? She picked up a stone, and now it's imbedded. I'll be digging it out later this afternoon. Want to help?"

"I don't know if you'll believe me," Lucy said at bit defensively, "but I can feel her pain."

"Why wouldn't I believe you?" answered Sylvester. "What a gift you have! I'm envious!" He smiled.

"My father never believed me. I never told anyone else. I figured they'd just laugh at me as well. But," Lucy hastened to say, "it isn't like telepathy with dragons. Esmeralda sends real words into my head."

Sylvester nodded. "I figured you'd be another non-rider who can communicate with dragons."

"With other animals, like your cow or my moles," she said smiling, "it's more like I pick up on what they're feeling. I can feel her pain in her rear left leg."

"Spot on," Sylvester said. "Hans is right. We're going to work well together. Let me finish walking you around. We'll find you a pair of scrubs and then help poor Nellie."

By the end of her two hours, Lucy was exhausted but happy. Sylvester had let her calm and comfort Nellie and even hold her foot up as he worked. She was pleased that he felt she'd been a real help.

I'm going to like working as his apprentice, Lucy mused as she walked home. *Home,* she thought. *This is home.* Even as tired as she was, there was a spring in her step as she walked into Amy's kitchen that evening.

— 12 —

INTERRUPTIONS

Lucy's first week of school at Havenshold was fun. Her life had changed so much, and she and Gretchen were becoming good friends. Of course Lucy knew everything would shift again if a baby dragon picked Gretchen, but that was still two weeks off. For now Lucy was happy.

School had really made a difference in her life and how others saw her as well. On Wednesday Miss Raven had Gregory in as a guest speaker to teach the students about the volcano. He was a natural-born teacher and enthralled the class. Lucy got really nervous when he called her up to the front of the room and told everyone about the moles and how Lucy's information gathering had helped him calm the volcano. Lucy refused to look up while he was telling the story, but when he finished and the class was absolutely silent, she glanced up to see everyone staring at her, but in a *good* way.

One boy raised his hand, and when Gregory called on him, he asked Lucy, "Can you talk to all animals?"

Gregory looked at Lucy. "Well, not exactly," she said. "It's more like I can sense their feelings and send feelings back to them."

There were a lot more questions, and Lucy was mortified that they were all for her. *Shouldn't they be asking Gregory about his amazing talk?* she wondered. *Will he be hurt that I'm hogging the questions?* She glanced at Gregory and saw that he was smiling.

After that Lucy had lots of students eating lunch with her.

Thursday morning, right after Miss Raven had set the class to work, Sylvester came hurrying in and asked her if he could take Lucy out of class for an emergency. Miss Raven nodded, and out Lucy went.

"What's wrong?" Lucy asked, as they rushed into the animal clinic.

"Farmer Holdsome just brought in his eight-year-old daughter's small nine pound dog, a orangey ball of fluff. When Farmer Holdsome was in the barn milking a cantankerous cow, the dog ran in and got too close. The cow kicked her clear across the barn. She's badly hurt, but I can't tell exactly where. Everywhere I touch her, she whimpers. I know there's internal bleeding, and Farmer Holdsome is no help at all. He keeps moaning and saying, 'What will my daughter do if Ginger dies?' "

"I'll do what I can," Lucy said.

As soon as they walked into the emergency room where Farmer Holdsome was standing helplessly next to his daughter's beloved dog, Lucy felt Ginger's pain and her absolute terror. Lucy started with calming thoughts aimed at the dog, letting her know they were trying to help her. As Lucy got close enough to put her hand on Ginger's head, she was able to sense where the pain was coming from, and Ginger calmed down a little. She was still obviously in pain, but Lucy was able not only to soften the pain but also relieve most of the fear. "She has some internal bleeding. Doesn't seem to be a lot, but definitely some. It's in the kidney region," Lucy reported. "And her back right leg may be broken." Farmer Holdsome let out a sob as he heard this.

"OK," Sylvester said. "That really helps." He shouted for Rose, who rushed in. "Rose, would you please take Farmer Holdsome out into the waiting room and get him a cup of coffee or tea?"

"Certainly." She gently but firmly guided the farmer out of the emergency room.

Sylvester sedated the dog, and with Lucy guiding him from her monitoring of Ginger, he was able to find the damage and repair it. Thankfully it was minor. He then examined the leg and confirmed Lucy's appraisal. Soon Ginger was sporting a blue cast on one leg and purple stitches on her belly. When she woke up, she seemed much happier. Sylvester had given the dog a shot of pain medication as well as an antibiotic.

As soon as Ginger was awake, Sylvester and Lucy called Farmer Holdsome in. Tears ran down his face as he thanked them. "Ginger means everything to my daughter. Thank you so much!"

"Well, just keep her out of the barn from now on," Sylvester said, and he nodded to Lucy. "You can head back to school before Miss Raven comes after us. Thanks so much for all your help."

Lucy smiled as she left. *It was wonderful to have been a part of that healing,* she thought, as she got back down to her math.

On Friday, right after lunch, William came into the classroom. He walked a bit hesitantly but nevertheless approached Miss Raven with his request. Lucy realized that Miss Raven probably had taught William before he had become a Dragon Rider. There was murmuring between them, and then Miss Raven called Lucy up to her desk.

"It's a good thing you're such an excellent student. It seems that once again you're being removed from my class. Somehow I doubt you'll be back today. Here's your homework for the weekend." Miss Raven handed Lucy a piece of paper.

"Thank you," Lucy said, not at all sure why William was here. She gathered her things, slung her backpack over her shoulder, and followed William outside. "Is something wrong? Is someone hurt?" Lucy asked anxiously.

"No, nothing like that," William said. "Let's head to my cave, where I can explain why I took you out of class." He was walking so fast that Lucy had a hard time keeping up. He was brimming with excitement.

Soon they were entering William and Thunder's cave, and Lucy saw the lovely brown dragon curled up in a giant bed in the corner. It was Lucy's first look at a rider home, and she noticed that William had a bed right next to Thunder's that was unmade, with some quilts thrown randomly across it. There was a desk across from the beds and a washstand in between. It looked as if someone had tried to decorate the walls with hangings, but Lucy suspected that was his mother's touch or possibly Amy's or both mothers together. Clothes were piled on top of the unmade bed as well. Then Lucy noticed that a large round hole had been made in one wall so that this cave linked easily with the next one. Lucy realized that the other cave must be Jake's. *So that's how they work partner housing when the riders are both still on active duty,* Lucy thought.

William found a stool tucked away in the corner, placed it next to his desk, and indicated that Lucy should sit there. "I don't know what, if anything, you know about me so far, other than that I am Jake's partner and hence Emily's brother-in-law. Thunder and I graduated in the same rider class as Emily and Esmeralda. That was just before Baron Geldsmith started his bid for the throne."

Lucy nodded, confused but interested.

William continued, "As a result of that uprising, I started studying telepathy more closely. I was intrigued while I was still an apprentice, but Clotilda gave me a full-speed-ahead assignment when she was head rider. Since then I've discovered that the Dragon Riders—and indeed all telepathic beings—used to have much stronger skills, like five hundred years ago when the riders first got to Draconia and met up with the gryphon, unicorn, and dolphin riders. Over the centuries, however, those skills have weakened. When I became a rider, everyone thought communication was limited to the rider and his or her bonded partner."

William stopped to take a breath, ran his hands through his hair, and looked very serious. "We've found out that isn't true. We now have a committee studying telepathic communication, and I'm the representative from Draconia. We have people who can send thoughts to unicorns, dolphins, or gryphons, and vice versa. Some can communicate over large distances, and we're trying to improve that as well. And some non-riders—like you, Gregory, and Sylvester—can hear thoughts from dragons."

"OK, but why did you need to get me out of school?" Lucy asked in a puzzled voice. She quickly added, "Not that I don't appreciate it."

"Because," continued William in a tone of voice that indicated he thought it was the most obvious thing in the world, "*you* are different. You're the first person we know of who can pick up thoughts or feelings of *non*-telepathic beings, such as moles. I want to try to figure out what you're doing and see if it doesn't somehow tie into telepathy. Will you help?"

Lucy sat back and nearly fell off her stool. She was stunned that William thought she could be of value in his work. She thought for a few moments, processing it all. "You know," she said finally, "since I've come to Havenshold and people have started to believe me about my communication with other species, I've noticed that my abilities seem to have gotten stronger. Yesterday, with Ginger, and earlier in the week with Nellie, I actually *felt* their pain in a specific location rather than just the generalized feelings I've usually gotten before, and I've never felt anything like that from moles or such before."

"I'm right!" crowed William. "These abilities *can* be strengthened. I need to clear it with Hans and Miss Raven, but if you're willing, I'd love to meet with you on a regular basis. Maybe we could make this one of your classes. I know Miss Raven said you've already completed all the graduation requirements Draconia expects before becoming a full apprentice, so we should be able to add it on. Maybe you could come here first and, after an hour, head off to Miss Raven's class. How does that sound?"

"It sounds absolutely wonderful!" Lucy said with a big smile. "This means so much to me—to have others recognize and trust in my abilities instead of being ridiculed and called a liar. And if I work with you in a class during school hours, I can still be faithful to my apprenticeship with Sylvester."

"OK, let me talk to Miss Raven, and I'll let you know over the weekend what we work out. I'm sure Jake and I will be over sometime to see the chaos with the sandpit, so we can help keep an eye on Todd." He finished with a smile. "And thanks," he added, as he walked Lucy back to the courtyard so she could go on to the animal clinic.

— 13 —

A FAMILY

Lucy woke up on Saturday morning and realized she was very glad it was the weekend. True, she still had her duties at the animal clinic, but Sylvester had said he didn't need her until ten, so at least it was better than a school morning. She was looking forward to Sunday, when she'd meet the rest of Emily's family.

Lucy took a shower, dressed, and headed down to breakfast. Amy looked up from the kitchen table when Lucy walked in, and she seemed so happy to see her. "I'll have your breakfast ready in a few minutes. Wasn't sure just what time you'd be down. While you're waiting, why don't you step out into the backyard and see how Chaosville is coming along?"

Lucy laughed and said, "I could help you, or even make my own breakfast."

"No, but thanks," Amy said. "I'll use any excuse to stay out of that mess. You'll see what I mean as soon as you step outside."

Lucy went through the kitchen door to the backyard and stopped dead in her tracks. There were six dragons out there digging. Gregory was directing, showing them just where and how deep to dig. Robert was detailing where the mounds of dirt should be placed. Hans, Jake, Emily, and William stood watching, each with a big mug of coffee in hand. And last, but definitely not least, was Todd, pacing back and forth nervously and making very unhelpful comments.

Todd saw Lucy first and came racing over. "Have we stayed away from the mole tunnels?"

Lucy laughed. "I'll go over to the bench and see if I can pick up anything from the moles, but I think you're fine."

"Thanks," Todd said then raced off to pace some more.

Lucy walked over and sat down on the bench at the edge of the pasture. She wasn't sure she could hear the moles over all the digging, but she was determined to try. Not only had Todd asked her, but also William had stressed how important it was to keep pushing the limits of her communication skills. She closed her eyes so she could focus and not be distracted by the three-ring circus in front of her. After about five minutes, she thought she sensed something—yes, there were the moles. They had gone a bit deeper, but they didn't seem to be in any distress; they were more curious than anything. She opened her eyes and found Todd.

"I think they're fine, Todd," Lucy reported. "I wouldn't come any farther this way if you don't have to, and I like that the dirt is being taken out into the low field. I'm sure the moles will be happy."

"That's great," Todd said. "Amy wanted more space to grow veggies, and that low patch has lousy drainage, so Robert suggested the dirt could be used to enrich that patch while we have a dragon sandpit here. Everyone seems happy about it all. To think it all started with your finding *moles*."

Lucy smiled. "Who knew, right?"

Amy came out with an enormous tray filled with platters and plates. She set in on a table just outside the kitchen door and called out, "Anyone hungry?"

Lucy laughed as everyone dropped what they were doing and hurried over. Amy filled a plate with scrambled eggs and toast and handed it to Lucy. "Better take this while there still is some. The rest of them are on their *second* breakfasts."

Once Emily had filled her plate, she came over to sit with Lucy. "How's your week been? Sorry I haven't been able to check on you, but I hear you're in good hands."

"Oh, yes," Lucy said. "It's been a wonderful week. My arm is healing well. Dr. Brian says the stitches can come out in another week, but he's thrilled by how it's looking, and I'm happy because it doesn't hurt anymore."

"I'm so glad," Emily said. "And how's school? How do you like Miss Raven? You know, we all had her as our teacher, even Hans. She's run our grammar school for nearly forty years."

"She's kind and seems pleased with me. She told William I'd already completed all the graduation requirements, and I still have a year-and-a-half left. Mr. Jones had always allowed me to work at my own pace and I guess my old school wasn't so bad as far as the academics went. I never let my father know that I was so far ahead because I didn't want to graduate any sooner than I had to, but now, that's all changed. And I made a friend, Gretchen, who's from my village. She never talked to me before because she didn't want to attract the bullies. She's a Dragon Rider candidate, so if she's picked next weekend, I won't see much of her, but at least we have another week before then. I really do hope she's picked, no matter what."

Emily smiled. "Next weekend will be exciting. You'll meet my sister Hannah tomorrow. She can't wait for the upcoming hatching."

Lucy looked puzzled. "Why? She already has her own dragon, Firebird."

Emily chuckled. "Dragon apprentices serve for nine years before graduation, just like other apprentices, but since there's a new group every three years, the most boring, dirtiest tasks always go to the youngest riders. For now that's Hannah and her fellow classmates, but next weekend they'll be the middle group, neither the youngest nor the oldest. She thinks it'll be better, but really it's done pretty fairly, and everyone takes their turn learning everything."

"They're so lucky," Lucy said.

Emily nodded. "I agree, but there are plenty of other great professions. Do you know that Gregory's dad wanted him to be a rider, but Gregory always wanted to be a volcanologist? He wished hard *not* to be chosen. He loves dragons, but that wasn't his path. The same with two of my brothers, Robert, the mad architect over there, and Michael, the botanist, whom you'll meet tomorrow."

"I guess," Lucy said, looking down at her right arm.

They both looked up when they heard Gregory shout, "Stop!" He continued, "OK, this is as deep as we want to go. I don't want to break through into the vent. I just want to put some rods in about a foot apart each. Robert, do you have those?"

Robert came over with a big bundle of short rods. "Here they are. I put ventilated covers on each end so they wouldn't fill up with dirt or sand."

"OK, everyone listen up! First rake this pit so that it's relatively flat. Then I want these rods placed in the ground along this line," he said, pointing to a string he had stretched across the pit. "Take a small trowel and dig a short hole. Place the rods in until about two-thirds of their length is buried, leaving the last third sticking out. Any questions? OK, let's do it."

Emily and Lucy stood up from the table and hurried over to join the work party. Soon everyone was laughing and having a good time.

Sure is fun to work when you have others to help, thought Lucy, as she got her third rod properly placed. It didn't bother her at all that she was slower, having to work one-handed, since no one else seemed to notice or care. Before long all the rods were positioned.

Robert said, "We need the boards placed next." He showed everyone just what he wanted so that everything would be stable and the sand would stay in the pit. Lucy worked with Jake this time, moving and positioning boards. "Pretty crazy family, huh?" Jake asked.

Lucy laughed. "Pretty wonderful!"

"Who's on the sand brigade?" Hans asked.

His father answered, "All you strong, young guys. The dragons already did their part bringing the sand and digging the pit."

William laughed. "Figures," he said, as he went with Hans and Jake. The three guys dragged the bags of sand into the pit and spaced them out. Then everyone got to work ripping bags and dumping sand. Emily checked surreptitiously on Lucy and was amazed to see how clever Lucy was at managing to rip open and dump a fifty-pound bag of sand by herself. Emily thought, *I can't wait to see what she does when she gets some of Nurse Beatrice's special tools.*

Lucy looked at her watch and realized she had to get to the clinic.

"Good timing," Emily said. "Sylvester won't be half as hard to work for as these guys. Esmeralda and I will give you a ride so we can get out of here too. They'll be at this all day. By the time we have Sunday dinner, I bet it'll be wonderful. Come on. Let's go."

The weekend flew by. Lucy really was enjoying her apprenticeship with Sylvester, and she was finding it easier and easier to get around Havenshold. By Sunday afternoon the dragon pit was completed, just as the rest of the family—Michael and Hannah—arrived for dinner. Lucy enjoyed meeting both of them. Michael took after Todd in appearance and Hannah was a smaller version of her mother. And as had been true with the rest of Emily's family, they were warm and friendly and easy to like, treating her as one of them immediately. She liked the entire family, and what seemed stranger to her was that they all seemed to like her as well.

Before dinner everyone went outside so Todd could explain the virtues of the sandpit. Of course seeing the six dragons stretched out and happy did make the benefits rather obvious. There were two greens, Fern and Jupiter; two browns, Harmony and Thunder; an orange, Fire Dancer; and a purple, Esmeralda. As everyone admired the dragons, Hannah whispered to Lucy, "After graduation I'll be able to bring Firebird, and that'll make *another* orange."

As they went inside for dinner, William and Hans caught up with Lucy and pulled her aside. Hans said, "William has talked to me about a special class for you on interspecies communication, and Miss Raven has assured me that she finds this to be an excellent opportunity for you. So, starting tomorrow, you'll have your first class at William's office then head off to Miss Raven. Does this sound agreeable?"

"Oh, yes," Lucy said enthusiastically. *If I can't be a rider, well, I'll still be able to work with dragons and help!* she thought. *I know I'll be taken on more rides.*

As everyone gathered around the large dining room table for a wonderful meal, Lucy knew she had found a family at last.

— 14 —

THE EGG THAT WOULDN'T HATCH

Lucy wasn't sure where the next week went. It seemed to speed by. She loved her class and work with William, and she was discovering that not only could Thunder speak telepathically to her, but she also could send a few thoughts back to him. It wasn't quite as easy yet as it was with Esmeralda. Lucy was beginning to realize that dragons were different from each other with their own personalities, just as people were. In fact, she was beginning to think that each dragon was very like his or her rider, or vice versa. Thunder seemed to be nearly as excited as William was about the research and she just enjoyed their enthusiasm.

Miss Raven was expanding Lucy's horizons as well. She'd finished all the history of Draconia and was now learning about the other three nations in their world, Forbury and the gryphons, Granvale and the unicorns, and Sanwight and the dolphins. Miss Raven couldn't believe how fast Lucy read and absorbed everything, but Lucy was thrilled to have the chance to really study. History was just one subject she loved. She was zooming through several other advanced subjects as well, and it was fun.

Lucy and Gretchen spent their lunches together, and Lucy treasured their growing friendship. After school it was off to Sylvester and the animal clinic. It had been a relatively quiet week at the clinic, so Sylvester encouraged Lucy to practice communicating with the horses and other animals. He loved to watch her, and he found it fascinating to learn more about the animals in his care.

Then, all of a sudden, it was the winter solstice, and every-thing in Havenshold stopped for the Dragon Hatching Festival. Lucy was pleased to be able to attend with Emily and her fam-ily. Hans was sitting in the celebrity box with the monarchs and dignitaries from all four nations. Jake, who was in charge of all the apprentices, and Hannah, currently his assistant, were with the Dragon Riders, who were involved with various duties, mak-ing sure everything ran smoothly.

As Lucy, Emily, and the rest of the family walked toward the hatching pit and the surrounding stands, Lucy was amazed at all the booths. There were food booths and craft booths and even some rides off to the side. She never had experienced anything like this before. She was so excited!

Emily's family took their seats, and Emily explained to Lucy exactly what would happen. First the candidates filed in and sat in a circle around the edge of the pit. Each wore a really thick, white robe, and Emily explained that the robes were insulated so that the heat of the sands wouldn't burn them. Each can-didate also had a lunch pail, which Emily said held a breakfast for the newly hatched dragons, who were ravenous when they hatched.

Lucy noticed there were twenty candidates but only thirteen eggs. She knew that by the end of the hatching she wouldn't be the only one disappointed not to be a Dragon Rider. Lucy found where Gretchen was sitting and managed to catch her eye with a wave. She hoped her friend would be one of the lucky ones.

As soon as everyone was seated, an expectant hush fell over the crowd. The stands around the hatching pit were completely packed. Everyone was waiting for the hatching to begin. Lucy found the hatching to be absolutely fascinating. An egg would start to crack, rocking back and forth. The candidates had to sit absolutely still. They weren't allowed to do anything that might influence the baby dragon. The choice of rider was entirely up to the dragon. Then, to complete the bond, the rider brought out food for the baby, signaling the rider's acceptance of the bond, and the rider then announced the dragon's name to the crowd, a name the dragon had spoken telepathically to her or his new rider. Lucy was interested to notice that the gender of the rider didn't necessarily match that of the dragon. After that the new pair was escorted from the pit to the caves for new riders. Lucy noticed that Jake and Hannah were on that escort duty.

Lucy thought it was comical to watch the baby dragons break loose from their eggs, then silently totter or stagger to their rider. She saw that some dragons nearly ran to their rider, while others wobbled around a bit hesitantly at first before making their choice. Emily explained that the candidates—all of whom were twelve to fourteen years old—had been tending the twelve-inch eggs, turning them and watching over them, for the past month so the baby dragons could get a sense of who the candidates were.

What an amazing process, thought Lucy, as yet another baby, this time a baby green, found his rider, a small blond boy.

A red dragon had just hatched and seemed to be heading toward Gretchen's part of the circle. Lucy found herself urging the red to pick Gretchen. Sure enough, her friend was the red dragon's choice, and Gretchen looked thrilled and, at the same time, awestruck and terrified as she quickly opened her lunchbox and started to feed her baby dragon. "Her name is Ruby!" Gretchen called out proudly.

Lucy didn't know any of the other candidates except by sight, as they were all her classmates. She saw panic creeping across the candidates' faces as the number of eggs decreased. Soon there was just one egg and eight candidates. Lucy figured they all must be thinking that the odds definitely weren't good.

A few minutes passed, but the last egg wasn't hatching. Lucy wondered, *What if it's a dud?* Apparently Hans was concerned as well, because he and Fire Dancer went down to the pit to check on the egg. Emily explained that if the egg were defective, it would have to be destroyed.

Fire Dancer communicated with the dragon inside the egg, and then Hans reported, "There's a fine, blue dragon inside, but she says she won't hatch until her rider is here."

Everyone exchanged puzzled looks. There were still eight candidates. What could the dragon mean? And could an egg refuse to hatch? Suddenly Lucy bolted upright. *No,* she thought. *I couldn't have heard that.* But there came the voice again— *Don't you want me?*

Lucy looked at Emily. "Did you hear that?" Lucy asked her.

"What?" Emily said. "I didn't hear a thing."

"I heard a dragon in my head...asking if I wanted it," replied Lucy with a trembling voice.

Immediately Emily jumped up, grabbed Lucy's arm, and hustled her down the aisle and into the hatching pit. Hans looked at them and said, "What do you think you two are doing here?"

But he had no sooner asked when the egg gave a loud crack. Emily pushed Lucy onto the hot sand. She quickly snatched off her coat and folded it so Lucy could sit on it to be protected from the heat. As soon Lucy sat down, a small bright-blue dragon climbed out of the egg and came straight at her, tipping over in her haste into Lucy's lap.

I'm Harriet, said the blue in Lucy's mind. *I'm so glad you came. I waited for you. I'm hungry.*

Lucy looked up at Emily and saw that Amy had followed them down as well. "Her name is Harriet, and she's hungry! I don't have any food." Tears welled in Lucy's eyes.

Hannah raced up to them. She'd been watching from the pathway to the new dragon caves, ready to escort the last rider. When she saw Lucy being dragged into the pit, she guessed what might happen and hurriedly had grabbed a bowl of dragon breakfast. She handed it to Lucy, and Lucy, with her right arm snuggled around Harriet, picked up the gravy soaked one-inch cubes in her left hand and began to feed Harriet.

Murmurs of protest rose in the crowds. Hans called Emily over and said, "What do we do now?"

Emily said, "How about congratulating Lucy?"

"But she wasn't an *official* candidate. I expect that murmuring will get louder and nastier. It was probably started by the parents of the remaining eight candidates," he answered. "I've never heard of anything like this before."

"Neither have I," Emily said, "but Harriet was definite. The dragon *always* chooses."

Hans nodded. He looked up into the stands, thought for a minute, then made his decision. "May I have everyone's attention? This is an unusual situation," he began.

"You aren't following the rules!" shouted an unsuccessful candidate's parent.

"This is irregular, for sure. I would like to ask for your patience while we sort this out. Amy will stay with Lucy and Harriet here in the hatching pit until a decision is made." He looked at his mother, and she confirmed with a nod that she would be happy to help. He continued, "I would ask that all dignitaries and monarchs follow Emily and me into my office, and we'll discuss this situation. Everyone else, please keep your seats until we return.

Or, if you would rather, you may exit the hatching pit and enjoy the many fine booths and entertainment opportunities outside. Thank you."

There was some underlying grumbling, but most people were just interested. A few folks left, but most were far too curious to move an inch. The remaining eight candidates sat perfectly still. Disappointment appeared on each of their faces, but they would stay put until all hope was gone. Everyone watched as the four monarchs and a few dignitaries filed out of the hatching pit.

Amy looked over Lucy's head at Emily. "What do you think?" she asked.

Emily looked down at Lucy and Harriet. "I think we have another Dragon Rider in the family," she answered, smiling. "I'd better catch up with Hans. Don't worry. I'll fight for them. They're meant to be together."

— 15 —

A QUANDARY

Hans was seated at his desk, and Emily—after scurrying around to find chairs for everyone—was seated next to him. Clotilda was on his right, and she looked very happy not to be in Hans's chair. Next to Clotilda sat Baron Geldsmith, then King Alfred from Forbury, then Queen Penelope from Granvale, and rounding out the semicircle, King Benjamin from Sanwight.

Hans began, "It seems we have a problem."

Baron Geldsmith spoke first. "What problem? The dragon picked her rider. Isn't that what's supposed to happen?"

"Yes," answered Hans. "But we've never had anyone picked who wasn't already a candidate. The candidates have been training for a month, so they know exactly what to do. Lucy didn't receive that training. She isn't a *qualified* candidate."

"Does that matter so much?" asked Queen Penelope. "We've had similar occurrences—not often, but still—and it seems to me the point of the hatching or birthing ceremonies is to allow the hatching or birthing individual to pick his or her rider with no pressure. The rider must confirm the bonding by feeding and also demonstrating a telepathic connection. Isn't this what happens in all of our ceremonies, no matter how they are accomplished?"

"You're correct, Queen Penelope, but—" started Hans.

The baron interrupted him. "Let's get to the real reason. You're worried because your rider is missing a hand. You don't think a cripple can become a Dragon Rider. That's your hang-up, isn't it? Do I have to remind you all of my story? After my *thankfully* aborted political coup, King Alfred took me to Forbury, and I was nearly bowled over by my wonderful Oswald. He had been born with only one wing and had the other one amputated for better balance. The important fact for this discussion is that Oswald knew me *instantly,* the moment I walked into the sanctuary. I, of course, knew nothing of him. So here I was, a forty-three-year-old man, bonded to a crippled baby gryphon, and I must say the two of us could not be better suited to each other or happier."

"Yes," Hans said, "but that was highly unusual."

King Alfred stepped into the discussion. "Yes, but when I saw Oswald racing over to the baron—and by the way, he did knock him over!—I knew without any question that the two had found each other and that it would be a strong symbiotic bond."

"Well," added King Benjamin, "maybe Hans is worried because, unlike Oswald, who was born without a wing and is lacking his full gryphonic abilities—"

The baron cut him off. "Oswald has all the abilities he needs!"

King Benjamin smiled. "Baron, I meant nothing disparaging about Oswald. I've met him, and he's wonderful, but Hans is now dealing with a *rider* with an impairment and a perfectly *healthy* dragon. Is that's what's bothering you, Hans?"

Clotilda said, "Yes, let's decide what the real problem is, or if there is a problem at all. Hans, what do you know of Lucy? I know your parents have taken her in as a foster, and I did meet her briefly after Emily and Esmeralda rescued her, but I know nothing else about her."

Hans thought for a moment before continuing. "I find Lucy to be incredibly resourceful, brave, and extremely bright. She has already, nearly two years early, finished her grammar school graduation requirements and is now moving into advanced studies with Miss Raven and William. She's able to work in Sylvester's animal clinic and knows more about most creatures than just about anyone. She's able to communicate with other species, maybe not entirely telepathically but enough to sense feelings, injuries, and so on and I honestly don't know how far she will be able to develop this skill. It will depend on whether the lack of telepathy with say moles and dogs etc. is because those species aren't telepathic, or because we haven't learned enough about them. Certainly, Lucy herself is highly telepathic since she could communicate from her first meeting with Esmeralda, something most non-riders are unable to do."

"Moles!" exclaimed King Alfred.

Hans smiled. "Yes, Lucy was sitting in our backyard and noticed that the moles nearby were thinking about warm earth. The quick version is that, thanks to her, pressure has been relieved on our volcano, and my parents now have a dragon sandpit in their backyard big enough for eight to ten dragons."

Clotilda said, "Well, it sure sounds to me as if Lucy is, if anything, *overqualified* for the position of Dragon Rider. What about her physical abilities?"

Emily looked at her brother, who nodded, so she said, "Lucy has had to learn to manage and has taught herself to do a remarkable number of tasks. When we found her, she was doing all the cooking and household chores for her father on their dairy farm, and she also was mucking out the stalls and feeding the cows daily. The only thing she couldn't do was the actual milking."

"Sounds very capable to me," said Queen Penelope.

Emily went on, "She did all that even though her amputation incision hadn't healed properly. Dr. Brian performed a minor surgery on it two weeks ago, and the stitches have just come out. In another couple of weeks, with some treatments, Nurse Beatrice will be able to fit her with a device that will allow her to use a variety of tools with her right arm."

"OK, the crowds are waiting for us. What then is the issue to be resolved, and how will we resolve it?" asked King Benjamin.

Hans said, "First and foremost is whether Lucy is physically able to raise a dragon. I gather the consensus here, from all we know about her, is a resounding yes." Everyone nodded. He went on, "Then there's the irregularity that Lucy wasn't an official candidate. It seems to me that the bonding ceremonies are always about the creature finding his or her rider. The bonds are always initiated by the dragon, gryphon, unicorn, or dolphin." Again everyone nodded. Hans continued, "And anyone present today could hardly doubt that Harriet picked Lucy. Harriet was so sure of her choice that she refused to hatch until Lucy was in the pit." Everyone nodded again. "I know there will be disappointed candidates and parents, but that's always the case. It's irregular, but there it is. Humans don't pick bonds, and we need to honor the bonds that are chosen for us. Let's go back out to the hatching pit, and I'll make the announcement."

Back in the pit, Hans looked at Lucy and Harriet. Lucy was cuddling the baby dragon, holding her in her right arm and petting her back with her left hand. Amy was watching over them both. Hans didn't think Lucy realized that anyone else was there.

"May I have your attention please?" Hans asked, and everyone was silent. "What happened today is unprecedented in Draconia, but I've heard from our fellow nations that they have had occasions where a rider was chosen who hadn't been an official candidate."

"Maybe, but was it a *cripple?*" someone shouted. Hans was sure he knew who that was. He had noticed a farmer in the back of the audience who seemed very upset. Hans glanced over at Lucy and saw the panic on her face.

She *knew* that voice. Amy quickly bent down to reassure her, and Lucy whispered, "That's my father! Why is he here?" Amy put her arm around Lucy, who was shaking.

Hans spoke loudly so everyone could hear him. "Many of you haven't had the opportunity to meet Lucy. Let me tell you a few things about her so you'll realize that Harriet chose very wisely when she selected her partner." Hans went on to list all of Lucy's qualifications, all the hurdles she had overcome, and the bravery she had exhibited. He talked about her being able to communicate with other species, her abilities to heal, the fact that she was nearly two years ahead in school, and so on. "As our own Queen Clotilda said, Lucy is far more qualified than any of our usual Dragon Rider candidates." He looked up at Lucy's father, as if daring him to contradict anything he'd said.

After some silence, Hans continued, "What many of us have lost sight of is the fact that riders don't chose their bond mates. In every case the dragon chooses the rider. The rider only agrees and seals the bond. Whatever happened, Harriet chose Lucy, refusing to hatch, as you all witnessed, until Lucy came into the pit, summoned by Harriet's telepathic call. That's all any of us needs to know. Lucy and Harriet are bonded."

Lucy was surprised to hear a loud roar of applause from the audience. Once Hans had told her story, the crowd was behind her. The disappointed candidates each came over to her and congratulated her and Harriet for finding each other. Lucy looked up to see her father leaving. She hadn't even known he would be here. What was wrong with him? But she had no time to think. Amy and Hannah were helping her stand as she held Harriet securely in her arms. They escorted her out of the hatching pit. Hans and Emily came up behind them and accompanied them as well.

"Mom, could I see you for a moment?" Hans said.

"Sure," Amy answered.

"Emily, Hannah, can you find a new cave for Lucy and Harriet?" Hans asked.

"I already found a great one," said Hannah enthusiastically. "It's the last of the new dragon caves and right next to the second class of riders—my class. I took the cave last in our line, so Lucy and I will be neighbors!"

Hans smiled, and Lucy looked very happy. After Emily and Hannah had escorted Lucy and Harriet off, Hans turned to his mother. "I have a favor to ask of you," he said.

Amy smiled. "You want me to watch over Lucy and Harriet?"

Hans nodded. "Lucy is overqualified in some ways. She won't need most of the Dragon Rider education. She's already learned all the book learning and then some, and she has a lot of experience with cows, sheep, dogs, cats, and so on, but she's never worked with dragons. I don't think our usual apprenticeship will fit her, and I don't think Sylvester and William want to lose her. Any ideas?"

"I was thinking about that actually. I think she should stay here in the new rider caves until Harriet can feed herself, and better still, fly. A few years should do it. For the first six months, Lucy will have a full-time job with Harriet, but after that, when the rest of the dragon apprentices start to attend classes, I'd have Lucy work with William and Sylvester. William can help her with the ins and outs of being a Dragon Rider, while they work on communication skills, and Sylvester can teach her about Dragon Rider equipment and dragon health and care while she's at the animal clinic."

Hans replied, "I like that. We can refine the plan further as Lucy progresses. I also like having them stay in the caves. Lucy needs more friends. I thought at first about sending them out to Dad's new sandpit and having you watch over her, but I think that would be too isolating. If you wouldn't mind stopping by every day, at least until Lucy learns the ropes, that would help. In addition to her physical disability, she also missed the month of training everyone else had."

"What was that with her father today?" Amy said. "Why did he show up? I don't know if he's a threat to Lucy, but I'd like to be sure we keep an eye on her without rattling her too badly. She was very shaken when her father yelled from the stands."

Hans answered, "I already have riders out looking for him."

"Thanks, Hans," replied Amy. "I imagine you have dignitaries to see to. If you run into your father, let him know I'm in Lucy's cave helping her settle in."

Hans headed back into the crowds, and Amy hurried to the caves.

— 16 —

BONDING

When Amy walked into Lucy and Harriet's cave, she nearly burst out laughing. Lucy and Harriet were cuddled in a large dragon nest filled with quilts, oblivious to all the activity around them.

Jake stood in the middle of the cave, his arms loaded with Lucy's things, and William was similarly encumbered. Someone, probably Hannah, had sent them home to gather Lucy's belongings. Hannah was putting things away in the small chest of drawers. Once Jake and William had been divested of their burdens, they walked over to stand next to Lucy and Harriet, both men smiling and looking really pleased. Hannah finished stashing stuff then spread out Lucy's quilt on her bed, although for the first six months most riders slept with their dragon in the nest.

Amy started to move in that direction when Emily came rushing in. Amy smiled. Her family certainly was taking excellent care of the new rider and her dragon. Lucy finally looked up to see them all staring at her.

Lucy beamed back at them and said, "Harriet likes me! She's *happy* here."

"And why wouldn't she be?" Emily said. "She couldn't have found a better rider."

Hannah nodded. "She's beautiful—such a lovely blue, rich and deep, but not too dark. Just right, I'd say."

Jake said, "She's smaller than the usual hatchling. I'd guess her to be about eight or nine inches rather than the usual twelve."

Lucy looked concerned. "But she's OK, right?"

William laughed. "Don't let Jake worry you. He just likes facts and figures. Harriet is perfectly healthy. Hans and Fire Dancer determined that before she hatched."

"That's right," said Hans, as he entered the cave. He was followed a couple of minutes later by Sylvester, who looked a bit sheepish and hesitant as he saw how full the small cave was becoming. Gregory was with him.

"Move on in, you two. You're blocking the doorway," said Todd, who was followed by Robert and Michael.

Lucy looked amazed. "Harriet just said I have a really big family."

"You do," Todd said. "We're all thrilled that you have Harriet now too."

Robert spoke up. "I expect you'll have us hanging around when we aren't busy. This is so exciting."

After everyone had gotten a good look at Harriet, Amy suggested they give Lucy some quiet time. "Why don't you all head out to the booths and find some lunch? And will one of you bring Lucy and me something to eat?"

"OK," Michael said. "I get to bring Mom and Lucy's lunch." No one argued as the cave emptied out.

Amy showed Lucy the amenities in the tiny cave. "You and Harriet will be together all the time for about the first six months. These new rider caves have a sink in the corner and also a small woodstove so you can cook your own food. Harriet will be eating baby dragon food until she's old enough to consume larger chunks and ultimately catch her own meals, but the kitchens cook that up by the gallons, and someone will stop by with food every few hours at first. All you have to do is snuggle and pamper yourself and Harriet."

Lucy glowed. "I've dreamed of this for so long, but I figured it was impossible." She looked down at her right arm. "This is more wonderful than I ever imagined."

Amy said, "I know. Believe me, all riders know there's nothing like this bond. Oh, here's Michael with our lunches."

Michael walked in hesitantly. "Thanks, Michael," Lucy said. They all ate in companionable silence.

"We'll give you two some peace and quiet. I'll check back before we leave the festivities," Amy said, as she and Michael headed out of the cave.

Lucy and Harriet snuggled in the dragon's nest and slept away the afternoon, with the only interruptions being feeding breaks.

Hans and Emily headed back to the office. Hans had sent out scouts to try to find Lucy's father and wanted to see if there were any reports yet. As soon as they opened the office door, they heard the shouting.

"I want to talk to someone fast! You have my daughter, and I want her back. I wasn't paid enough. I can't manage without her. You get her in here now," said the man, who was obviously the same man who had called Lucy a cripple at the hatching.

Hans stepped around to his desk and nodded at William, who'd been the target of all the yelling. "I'll take it from here, William. You may go. Thanks."

As William beat a hasty retreat, Hans turned to Lucy's father. "We haven't met, but you must be Eugene, Lucy's father. I've heard a lot about you." Hans deliberately didn't offer to shake hands. Emily moved around to sit beside Hans. "Won't you please be seated?" Hans said. "What can we do for you?"

"You can give me back my daughter!" Eugene roared.

Hans replied, "I have a copy of the papers you signed." He pulled some papers out of his file drawer. "They clearly state that you relinquished all rights to guardianship over Lucy and assigned that guardianship over to the Havenshold Dragon Riders. Specific mention is made that Lucy would be fostered with Amy and Todd Morris. If Amy and Todd are unable to continue as foster parents, new foster parents will be chosen from among the Dragon Riders. For this relinquishment of Lucy's guardianship, we paid you an amount equal to three years' profits on your dairy farm. This is all quite clear and legal."

"I don't know about that," snarled Eugene. "She *tricked* me," he said, pointing at Emily. "I need Lucy to cook and clean for me. My wife died saving her. That girl owes me."

Emily started to snap back, but Hans put his hand out to quiet her. He said quietly and firmly, "Lucy doesn't owe you a thing. On the contrary it is *you* who owe *her.*"

Eugene yelled, "What do you mean? I kept a roof over her head, didn't I? And I fed her all these years."

Hans continued, "What any parent owes to any child they bring into this world is love—a safe and nurturing environment. Lucy may have had this with your wife, but after the earthquake, you abused her in every possible way. We saw how you snatched her out of our hospital just two hours after her hand had been amputated and how you didn't allow her to have the proper treatment, which resulted in her needing a second surgery two weeks ago when she arrived here."

"Doesn't matter," snapped Eugene. "She's mine, and I mean to have her."

Hans replied, "Actually she is, thankfully, no longer yours. You signed away all your rights. We love Lucy. As you saw today, she's bonded to a lovely baby dragon. That makes her a full-fledged Dragon Rider. Even without your signed agreement, she leaves your custody the moment a dragon bonds with her."

"You Dragon Riders are all the same. You stole the love of my life. She had no business being picked. I've come to every hatching since then to try to stop this. Once my Mary went off with you people, I had to marry another so I'd have help on the farm. You think you're so grand, but you make a mess of folks' lives. And now you've stolen my daughter. You give her back *now*."

Hans concluded, "I'm sorry for your loss, but Dragon Rider candidates are always twelve to fourteen. How could you have picked someone to spend your *life* with at that young age? And how could you marry someone you didn't love? You have some major problems, but you won't drag Lucy back into them. Now she's free and happy."

"She doesn't deserve to be happy after she *killed my wife*," Eugene said.

"Enough!" Hans said in a loud voice as he stood up. "You poisoned Lucy with that kind of talk, and I'll hear no more of it. Your wife freely sacrificed her life for Lucy. She did it so Lucy could have a full and rich life. Lucy has that now, no thanks to you. I'm going to have you escorted out of Havenshold. You're never to return."

"You can't tell me what to do," blustered Eugene.

"I rule Havenshold, so I can tell you what you can do here. Queen Clotilda has met Lucy as well and has sworn to protect her outside of Havenshold if necessary. Get out of here, and be thankful Emily was so generous with you. I wouldn't have paid you anything."

Hans went to his door and spotted Jake and William in the outer office. "Will you two please escort Eugene to the edge of Havenshold and make sure he doesn't return?"

Both men nodded. "Our pleasure," Jake answered, as they took up positions on each side of Eugene.

"I'll get her back! Just you wait," yelled Eugene, as Jake and William each grabbed an arm and hustled him out of the office.

Hans went back in. Emily was red with anger. "That foul, vile man," she spluttered. "Lucy is amazing to have survived and to have become so sweet with that...*thing* for a father."

"Don't tell Lucy about this," suggested Hans. "I don't want anything to spoil this day for her."

Emily nodded. "Let's make sure that everyone knows who he is and that we'll protect Lucy and Harriet."

Hans agreed. "OK, enough business. Let's head back out, and I'll treat you to dinner before the fireworks. Maybe we can find the rest of the family and watch together. I bet Lucy and Harriet will sleep through it all!"

Emily walked out with Hans and said, "I'd better find Gregory. He'll be wondering where I've gotten to."

— 17 —

APPRENTICESHIP

The weeks and months rolled by quickly. Lucy couldn't believe how big Harriet had gotten. By the end of six months, she was eight feet long! She still was smaller than the other dragons, but Lucy didn't care. Harriet was also very smart. Lucy thought she was the smartest dragon ever, of course, but even the other riders had to admit that Harriet picked up on things—like hunting—faster than most of the other dragons. An older rider mentored each new rider. Lucy seemed to be mentored not by *a* rider but by a *herd* of riders. Amy was her official mentor, even though she was a retired rider, but everyone else in the family felt it was their duty to mentor her as well, including Robert and Michael, who weren't riders at all. It was wonderful.

On Harriet's first birthday, the family had a party in Lucy and Harriet's cave. At the party, Harriet amazed them all, especially William, because she was able to speak telepathically with *everyone.*

"I've never heard of that before," William said in total amazement. "Many dragons won't communicate with anyone except their own rider. After the attempted coup, we've crossed that hurdle, so all but a few of the oldest dragons and riders will communicate telepathically with others, but dragons always take several years to be able to communicate completely with their own rider. Harriet, you are *fantastic!"*

Harriet responded so all could hear her, *Thank you, William. Lucy has been helping me learn.*

Lucy turned bright red and said, "It's really all your lessons, William. I'm practicing, and of course I'm with Harriet when I practice, so I figured we could learn together.

"You never said anything about it," William said.

"I wanted to surprise you," Lucy told him, and they all laughed.

The next several years flew by with Harriet growing at a terrific rate and Lucy caring for her as well as continuing her studies with William and Sylvester. At two years of age, Harriet was a full-size dragon. She was still smaller than average, but that suited Lucy just fine. She still was a *lot* of dragon when it came time to oil her scales with Harriet's favorite vanilla-scented oil.

At three years Harriet began to fly on her own over short distances. She loved to fly to Amy and Todd's so she could roll in their sandpit. While it was unusual for apprentices to be allowed to take their dragons out of the caves, Hans had made an exception for Harriet when he had made all the changes to Lucy's apprenticeship. Everyone was still worried that Lucy's father would show up, even after all this time, so both she and Harriet were watched carefully.

By the time Harriet was six and Lucy was nineteen, they started to fly together. Lucy felt like she had waited for this day all her life. Emily—and indeed all the riders in her family—had prepared Lucy by giving her rides and helping her mount and dismount their dragons. That certainly helped, but it wasn't the same as the real thing.

For their first flight, Harriet had crouched as low to the ground as she could and bent her front left leg. Lucy had raised her left foot to Harriet's bent knee and reached as high as she could onto Harriet's back, and then with a big push from her right leg, she hauled herself up and swung her right leg over. The first time was far from graceful, but all Lucy really cared about was that she had done it all by herself. *Well, all by ourselves,* thought Lucy, as she knew she never would have made it without Harriet's help.

Lucy and Harriet had just moved into their third cave. Every time a rider class graduated—this time it was Hannah's class— all the rider apprentices shifted caves so the new rider caves would be ready for the next hatching.

This time Lucy and Gretchen managed to snag neighboring caves. They were now in the senior class of apprentices. Hans had shifted Lucy's class schedule so she was now training with Gretchen and the others in her class for flying lessons. One day, when Lucy and Gretchen were out practicing by themselves, Gretchen suggested that Lucy could use her gymnastics training to vault onto Harriet. Gretchen demonstrated by vaulting onto Ruby.

"You make it look so easy," complained Lucy.

"It will be," assured Gretchen. "I've seen you in gymnastics, and you vault sublimely."

"Oh, yeah, right. Like the time I landed flat on my back," Lucy muttered.

"That was just once, and it was only because you had an audience. It's just us now and I promise I won't laugh if you don't make it," Gretchen said.

But you're the one I'd like to impress, thought Lucy. She hoped Gretchen didn't see her cheeks turn rosy.

Then we will, Harriet thought back to her. *I think Gretchen is right. I think you could do a running vault much more easily than clambering up me. You've seen Emily do it enough times on Esmeralda. Please! We can do it.*

Lucy laughed out loud. "OK, Gretchen. Harriet agrees with you. I'm sure glad this is a very soft, grassy field. Here goes."

To no one's amazement except Lucy herself, she landed a perfect vault right on top of Harriet. Gretchen cheered and had her try it several more times to build Lucy's confidence.

"We won't say anything to anyone, and tomorrow in class, you can vault onto Harriet as if you've been doing it all your life," Gretchen said.

"You're the *best* friend ever," Lucy said. This time Gretchen blushed.

That weekend the new seniors were allowed to fly solo for several hours. Gretchen suggested they fly back to Cliffside to say hi to everyone. Lucy knew Gretchen was dying to show off Ruby to her family and friends, but Lucy wasn't sure she wanted to go along. Lucy had written faithfully to her father every month for the last six years since she'd left home. She had all the letters in a drawer, all returned unopened. She hadn't heard from her father since the hatching, and as much as she understood his pain, she wasn't sure she wanted to see him.

Gretchen pleaded with Lucy. "You can stay with me. You don't have to go to your farm, but they said we couldn't go for more than an hour unless we paired up, and it takes *two* hours to fly to Cliffside. Please. It would mean so much to me. I really miss seeing my mother. My father died when I was a baby and since then it has just been mom and me. I know it is hard for her to have me gone. Please. Next time we get a weekend off, I'll go anywhere you want. I promise."

Lucy relented. First thing Saturday morning, they took off after logging their destination in the apprentice logbook. It was a beautiful morning, clear and crisp. Winter was coming, but it wasn't here yet. The trees below them were alight with fall colors. Lucy tried to relax and enjoy the flight, but she still felt apprehensive.

Remember, said Harriet, *I can breathe fire. I can protect you.*

That made Lucy laugh. Harriet finally had mastered fire breathing, or maybe "accomplished it" would be more accurate, because it was still very erratic. It had taken her longer than the other dragons, probably because of her size, so she was very pleased with herself now that she had managed it.

OK, Lucy thought back at her, *but don't burn Cliffside down, please.* This time it was Harriet who chuckled. Lucy enjoyed the rest of the trip. Soon they were landing in the street in front of Gretchen's house. Lucy had forgotten that there were very few spots for dragons to land in town.

Gretchen's mother, Nancy, came running out, and hugs were exchanged all around. Gretchen introduced Lucy and Harriet. Nancy insisted they stay for lunch, and they decided they could manage that before heading back. They had to be at Havenshold by dinnertime. Nancy was a heavy-set middle-aged woman with the same hair and eyes as Gretchen and just as big a smile. She ran the town's café and always had good homemade food on her menu. Nancy told her assistant to handle the lunch rush and the three of them sat in a booth at the back of the café. Over lunch Gretchen told her mom about their flight and how wonderful it was that Lucy had agreed to come so they could visit.

After lunch Lucy, Gretchen, Harriet, and Ruby walked down the main street. They chuckled at all the stares they got, but most folks waved and shouted out happy greetings. They remembered how much help the riders had been after the horrendous earthquake. As they walked past the schoolhouse, Lucy thought of all the bullying she had endured, but also all the knowledge she had gained in the hours she had spent there.

They were nearly past when Mr. Jones rushed out to meet them. He shook them both by the hand, remembering to do a left-handed handshake with Lucy, which surprised her. He admired both Harriet and Ruby, and Lucy noticed how handsome the blue and red dragons looked next to each other.

"Lucy, I owe you an enormous apology," Mr. Jones said. "I never noticed all the bullying you endured when you were a student here. Truly I didn't. I was so busy trying to make a go of it in a new school that I avoided anything that might smack of trouble. Your speech the day you left has haunted me. Now I'm much more vigilant. I hope I can say with honesty that our school is now a safe haven for *all* students, and that's thanks to you."

Lucy blushed and looked at the ground for a few moments. Then she looked up and said, "I had some pretty miserable years—not just at school—but if what I said has changed things so other students are protected, well, then I won't say it was worth it, but at least good has come out of my pain. Thank you for being willing to listen and make some changes." Lucy continued in a happier vein, "And they were amazed when I got to Havenshold about how far ahead I was! I want to thank you for all your encouragement with my studies."

"Thank you. I'd love to come to your graduation. Don't decide now. Just let me know when the time comes," Mr. Jones replied. He bid them a great day and returned to the schoolhouse.

"Whew," Gretchen said. "Never thought that would happen, but it's wonderful!"

Lucy nodded, and they continued to walk through town. The clinic was on the far side, on the way to Lucy's father's farm. She still hadn't decided about seeing her father, but she did want to see Marta.

As they reached the clinic, Gretchen said, "I can wait here with the dragons. You go on."

"I'll bring Marta out, and you can meet her. She's wonderful," Lucy said, as she turned to walk into the clinic.

As soon as Lucy opened the door, Marta yelled out screams of joy and charged at her, giving her an enormous hug. Lucy hugged her back then said, "Would you like to meet Harriet?"

"Lead on," Marta said, and they both came outside. Marta looked very pleased as Lucy introduced her to Harriet, Gretchen, and Ruby. "You Dragon Riders do so much good. Our town never could have recovered as quickly as it did without you. And look at you two with your gorgeous dragons! You're nearly finished with your apprenticeship. I'm so proud of you, Lucy! And you too, Gretchen," she added hastily. Marta turned to Lucy. "Remember that day when you came by on your way out of town? And you made that speech? Well, Dr. Penelope never would admit it to anyone—especially to you—but after that things slowly started to change here, and now you wouldn't recognize the place. Agnes has gone to another village. Dr. Penelope hired a *real* office manager who understands people. I won't say Dr. Penelope never explodes, but she works hard not to lose her temper, and if she does, well, the new manager calls her on it. You made a real difference here. It's helped all of us. Thank you so much!" She gave Lucy another hug.

Lucy and Gretchen got up on their dragons. Marta was so eager to see them fly, and they were ready to head back to Havenshold. Marta was really impressed with their vaults and said the two of them looked spectacular on their dragons. She waved as they took off.

Lucy realized they would have to fly over her father's dairy farm as they turned to head back to Havenshold. Gretchen had left it up to her as to whether or not they stopped. *Well, why not? Mr. Jones and Marta were happy we came. Maybe my father will be also,* Lucy hoped deep inside her heart.

They landed in the fields in front of the house, but before they could even get off of their dragons, Lucy's father stormed out with a shotgun in his hands. "You get out of here, you wretched ingrate." He fired a shot that went wild, but that was enough for Lucy. She signaled Gretchen, and up they went before he could fire again.

Lucy sobbed hard as they flew.

He doesn't deserve you, said Harriet.

Gretchen looked over at her friend and asked, "Would you like to stop somewhere before we get home?"

Lucy shook her head. "No, let's just get home as fast as we can. I never want to go back there again."

— 18 —

GRADUATION

Graduation was approaching faster than any of the riders in Lucy's class could believe. Nine years had zipped by. Now they had to prove themselves worthy of the title "Dragon Rider" and demonstrate a strong and constant bond with their dragons.

Hans had called Lucy into his office six months ago to discuss the ceremony with her. He had noted that for most of the riders an aerial dance was their final test as apprentices. They had to perform above the crowds solo for three minutes to demonstrate complete trust and skill with their dragon.

"I'm concerned this may be an unfair requirement for you," Hans had begun. "How do you feel about it?"

Lucy had looked across his desk and smiled. "Thank you, Hans, for caring and for worrying about me, but Harriet and I are confident that we can do an excellent aerial performance. Maybe others will be more spectacular, but we don't have to be the flashiest or the fastest. I think you'll be pleased with what we've planned."

Hans looked carefully at Lucy. Was this really the same person as that scared, injured teenager who had walked into their lives nine years ago? She was poised and self-confident, above average in height with a slim build. He noticed that she'd finally settle in to shoulder length hair after trying many styles. And most of the time, as long as the job didn't require it, she did not add any mobility aids to her right arm, just using it as naturally as if she'd never had a hand there. Looking at her now, Hans was convinced she could do just what she'd said. "Great, then," he said. "I'll look forward to watching you."

Since then Harriet and Lucy had practiced their routine during every spare moment. Lucy wanted to use scarves, and when she had mentioned this to Nurse Beatrice, Beatrice had promised her that she and Sylvester would design something to fit in her right arm holder that would work as Lucy wanted it to.

On the morning of graduation, Lucy groomed Harriet with oil until Harriet shone with her full radiance. They both had soaked for a long time in the riders' hot springs, and Lucy wanted to be sure they looked their best. Lucy was wearing lovely royal-blue slacks with a magenta top. Sylvester even had made her a pair of royal-blue boots that were supple and easy to run in. Gretchen stopped in at Lucy's cave to ask if Lucy wanted her to do her hair, and Lucy was happy to accept. Gretchen wove long blue ribbons into Lucy's mid-length brown hair. The ribbons would fly when Lucy and Harriet flew.

The young women looked at each other. Gretchen wore an entirely red outfit, and the top had red sequins. "You'll blind the audience with your magnificence," Lucy told her friend.

Gretchen smiled and said, "You don't look too bad yourself." Gretchen then helped Lucy check to make sure the blue holder on her right wrist fit perfectly, and Gretchen watched as Lucy snapped a series of clamps onto the holder.

"What's that for?" Gretchen asked. She hadn't seen any of Harriet's dance practices and was dying to know what Lucy would do.

"Just you wait and see," Lucy said.

All twelve of the graduating riders lined up with their dragons, ready for the processional. Lucy had to admit it was a most
impressive sight. They entered a large arena that was just outside the main courtyard to the north. A similar arena to the
south contained the hatching pit. In just three months, on the
winter solstice, a crowd would gather again for the next hatching, and so the cycle would continue.

Hans and Fire Dancer were waiting in the center of the arena
floor. The stands overflowed with spectators. Lucy looked
around and quickly spotted Hannah and Emily waving madly
at them. They were sitting with her entire family: Amy, Todd,
Jake, William, Emily, Gregory, Robert, Michael, and Hannah.
Of course the last member of her family was Hans, who stood
right beside her.

Gretchen caught her attention and said, "Look over there."

Lucy spotted Gretchen's mother, and then she did a double
take. It was Marta and Mr. Jones. They'd come! She smiled and
waved at them. She looked around again but wasn't surprised
that her father wasn't there. He was still returning her letters
unopened, but she never would give up. She wouldn't make
the mistake again of stopping at the farm until he communicated that he wanted to see her, but for her mother's sake she
would keep trying.

Hans started to speak. "Welcome, visiting monarchs and
dignitaries." He bowed to the box where all four monarchs were
seated, along with some other officials. "And welcome to the
families and friends of our latest graduating class. Finally, welcome to everyone who has come today to share in the celebrations for these fine young men and women who have worked
very hard for nine long years to attain the rank of Dragon Rider."

There were lots of shouts of congratulations and deafening applause. Hans held up his hands for silence. "As their last
act as apprentices, each pair will perform a three-minute aerial

dance for your enjoyment. The dances will demonstrate to us that each rider and dragon are a fully bonded pair, ready to take on the duties of a Dragon Rider." Hans turned to the riders. "Please move over to the side, and then in the order in which you are now lined up, take your turn and show us what you can do. Good luck to you all," he concluded, as he and Fire Dancer moved to the opposite side for the best view.

Lucy watched as her classmates performed one by one. They were chosen in the order of the rainbow, so Gretchen, as the rider of the only red dragon, was the first to perform. Since there were no purple dragons in this class, Lucy and Harriet would go last. As Gretchen headed out, Lucy wished her luck.

Gretchen and Ruby performed magnificently. Their dance was one of beauty and grace, as if they were performing a ballet in the air. Gretchen and Ruby swirled so fast that Lucy wondered how they kept from being too dizzy to move, and then the soared high into the sky before diving in a swoop. Lucy clapped wildly—as did the entire arena—as they landed, and she quickly congratulated her friend.

Lucy watched as the next ten riders performed. Some did spectacularly athletic dances, some did graceful ballets, and a few were able to combine the two skills into an athletic ballet. Each dance was unique and matched the rider-dragon pair perfectly.

As the last green dragon and his rider began their dance, Lucy quickly pulled a rainbow of scarves out of her left pocket and threaded them one by one into the clamps. She then dismounted Harriet so they would walk into the arena side by side. The other riders had all entered mounted, but then no one would ever question that they could mount and dismount unaided.

Lucy had taken Hans's talk to heart about this being the final test of worthiness, and she didn't want there to be any doubt in anyone's eyes that she was a fully qualified rider. She and Harriet each had to prove themselves—Lucy because of her missing hand, and Harriet because of her small stature.

With all eyes on them, Lucy led Harriet to the center then walked about fifty feet behind her. Harriet stood tall—well, as tall as her ten feet would allow, but even if she wasn't a full eighteen feet, she looked breathtaking. The sun shone on her, and her royal-blue scales were dazzling. Lucy was so proud of her.

Lucy bowed to Hans to signal she was ready to begin, and Hans nodded in return and flipped the timer. Lucy ran the fifty yards to Harriet at an astounding speed, broken only by a couple of flips in the air on the way. It was timed so perfectly that her third flip landed her perfectly centered on Harriet's back. The crowd gasped in amazement.

Harriet and Lucy took off nearly vertically into the skies and began their dance, which was definitely on the athletic side, although they were graceful. Again Lucy had decided that any naysayers would be wondering about her physical capabilities, so she demonstrated her skills to perfection, riding one-handed and flipping the scarves around in various patterns.

Then, as their time was running out, they flew over the royal box and spoke telepathically to each of the dignitaries, saying *Welcome!* and then *Catch!* as Lucy dropped the scarves one at a time above each monarch.

They still had one scarf left as they began their return to the stands. She and Harriet dropped the scarf neatly into Amy's lap as they flew just above the Morris family, and she said telepathically to the entire family, *I love you all. Thank you!*

Harriet and Lucy landed. The applause was deafening. She looked up at Hans, and his smile said it all. *We did it,* Lucy said to Harriet.

Did you have any doubts? Harriet chortled.

As the audience settled down, Hans called all the riders and their dragons to the center again. "You have all performed outstandingly and demonstrated that you are ready to join the ranks of Dragon Riders, with all the duties and privileges associated with that rank. Let me assure you that there are many more *duties* than *privileges*." Everyone laughed at that.

Hans and Fire Dancer presented each of the riders with a hand-woven scarf in the color of their dragon, and the dragons received a gold necklace with a stone in the center that matched their color. Hans stepped back from the riders and dragons and clapped. The audience quickly followed suit. Hans had the new riders lined up with their dragons in a receiving line so family and friends could congratulate them.

The monarchs and dignitaries started the congratulations. Lucy was touched that each of them stopped to give her a special word. "May wanted me to give you her best!" Clotilda told her. "You and Harriet certainly have proven that Harriet knew what she was doing when she chose you all those years ago. I've never had a dragon and rider speak telepathically to me in the middle of a dance! Amazing."

King Benjamin, King Alfred, and Queen Penelope made similar comments. They had been truly surprised by the words as the scarves floated down.

Last, but certainly not least, of the dignitaries was Baron Geldsmith. "I told them all they were fools for worrying about you," he said to Lucy. "Look at us—neither of us bonded in the traditional way, and both of us have fantastic bonds. Being different is nothing to worry about! I've kept up with your progress through my son, Gregory, and I must say that you and Harriet an astonishing pair."

Lucy turned bright red but managed to stammer, "Thank you, Baron."

Once the dignitaries had made their way through the receiving line, the families and friends were free to come up. There were so many well-wishers that it nearly became a mob scene.

Most people just made their way to a particular rider and dragon. However, Gretchen's parents stopped to congratulate Lucy and Harriet on their way to their daughter. Her mother said, "You two do Cliffside proud." Lucy thanked her.

Then Marta gave Lucy a big hug, and Mr. Jones shook her hand, and they both said how proud they were of her and how happy they were that she had finally found a safe, loving home. Lucy appreciated their words and felt this brought healing to them all.

Lucy and Harriet's family crowded around them. Finally Amy said, "OK, let's move this family party out into a bigger space."

Lucy noticed that many of the riders and dragons already had left the arena to join in the festival celebrations, and certainly she and Harriet were thankful to get out of the arena and all the attention.

The afternoon was wonderful. Lucy and Harriet basked in all the praise for their dance. Beatrice and Sylvester came up to congratulate Lucy and said how clever she had been with the clamps and scarves.

"We couldn't have done it without you," Lucy said with a smile.

"Are you going to be working more with me now that you don't have to practice so much?" Sylvester asked.

Before she could answer, William said, "Hey, she's going to be working more with *me*. That ability to communicate with the dignitaries telepathically while twisting and turning and releasing the scarves above them—that shows some serious ability. Most riders couldn't have done that kind of telepathy with their feet on the ground. We need to see how far Lucy's abilities can reach."

Lucy smiled at them both. "Let's work on some balance here. I love and enjoy working with you both. Give us some time to unwind, and then I think Harriet and I can satisfy everyone."

Sylvester and William had the good graces to look a bit sheepish, and soon everyone was laughing and heading to the food booths, where Hans joined them. Emily and Gregory already had marked out a large area on the grassy knoll just outside the arena. Soon all of them had gathered there to enjoy the sunny afternoon and await the spectacular fireworks that always ended the graduation festivities.

Lucy sat leaning against Harriet and said to her, *Isn't this the most wonderful thing in the world? I have you, and we have a family.*

Harriet, getting sleepy in the sun, said, *Nothing better.*

— 19 —

MINE COLLAPSE

Lucy and Harriet had settled into their new cave and their new lives as a Dragon Rider pair. They had spent their first few months touring schools in Draconia to speak out against bullying. Clotilda and Hans had asked if they'd be willing to be ambassadors for this. Of course they'd agreed instantly.

Most of their time was taken up working with William and Sylvester, who had managed to develop a workable sharing plan. Of course each of them was totally obsessed with their own work, and each wanted exclusive access to Lucy, but Lucy wanted to work with both of them and thankfully that was what happened. William had Lucy and Harriet in the morning, and Sylvester had them in the afternoon. William quickly realized that when Lucy and Harriet were with Sylvester, they were also practicing what William had suggested, so everyone was happy.

Lucy had learned she could communicate on at least a basic level with almost every species. She really wasn't sure about insects, but all mammals were relatively easy, and she'd even found a cat that could return the communication, which was really exciting. Sylvester had been operating on the cat, stitching her up after she'd been cornered by a raccoon, when Lucy realized she wasn't just calming the cat—a gorgeous brown tabby—but that she was answering the cat's questions.

Once the cat was through surgery and recovering satisfactorily, Lucy said, *Do you have a home?*

The cat responded rather morosely, *No, my person died last month. She was old, but I miss her.*

Lucy asked the cat if she wanted to live with them, and then she asked Harriet if that was all right. Then Lucy got her next shock. The cat, whose name was Sage, chatted telepathically with Harriet, and Harriet returned the compliment by answering her, as both Harriet and Sage agreed that this would be a good home for Sage. *Wait until William finds out about this!* Lucy thought, as she carried Sage back to their cave, where Harriet was sleeping in her nest. *The two of them hadn't even been in the same room,* thought Lucy, as she made a small nest for Sage then raced out to find William.

Lucy crunched through the new-fallen snow on her way to William's cave, but as she turned a corner, she nearly ran into Hans, who was hurrying to find her. "Quick," he said. "Come with me to my office. There's been a horrific mine collapse in Forbury. We need to send help."

Once Lucy and Hans reached his office, Lucy saw that Emily and Gregory were already there. As soon as Lucy and Hans were seated, Hans began, "We only have very sketchy details, but the main thing is that a very large copper mine collapsed in Forbury. King Alfred has asked for help. I don't know the full extent of the damage, but the king has put Baron Geldsmith in charge of the rescue, as he knows how to move earth and dig."

Gregory nodded. "Nothing like six months of having to work your way out of a blocked pass to teach you."

"Yes," Hans said, "and it certainly makes the baron well qualified for this rescue operation. We have no idea how many miners may be trapped. Your father asked for you specifically,

Gregory, as he wants to find out if the volcano is in any way to blame for the collapse. He asked for you as well, Lucy. He was really impressed with your demonstration of communication skills at your graduation four months ago, and he's hoping you'll be able to find out where any trapped miners might be. Emily, I want you to go as my representative. Gregory can ride with you on Esmeralda. Any questions?"

The three of them looked at one another and shook their heads. "No," answered Emily for them all. Then, looking at Lucy and Gregory, she said, "Grab lots of warm clothes and a couple pairs of boots at least. We'll need some food packs too. I'll see to them. Let's meet up in the central courtyard in an hour."

"Thanks, and good luck," Hans said, as the other three left. "Please keep me apprised of your progress."

"Will do!" shouted Emily, as they rushed to their quarters.

As soon as Lucy entered her cave, she remembered Sage. *What shall I do with her?* thought Lucy.

Take me, said Sage without any hesitation.

Harriet agreed. *She can travel in one of my saddlebags. She'll be warm and safe, tucked up in your clothes. Plus, if Sage can communicate with us, she might be of assistance in this rescue.*

Lucy smiled. She should have known Harriet would be one up on her, and of course Harriet was right. Sage was small and wouldn't be any trouble. Even if Sage couldn't help, she'd at least be with them, and they were a family now—a strange family but a family nonetheless.

Lucy packed quickly, put the saddlebags on Harriet, and loaded Sage into one of them, as Harriet had suggested. *You OK in there?* Lucy asked Sage.

Yep, answered the cat.

Lucy told them both to keep quiet about Sage for now. She didn't know how the other riders or dragons, even one as lovely and sweet as Esmeralda, would take to Sage.

They met up with Emily, Gregory, and Esmeralda in the central courtyard. After a few last-minute instructions from Hans, who had come out to see them off, they were airborne toward Forbury.

It took them about three hours to reach the accident site. As soon as they landed, Baron Geldsmith greeted them. "Thank you so much for coming so promptly," he began. "As you can see..." He waved his hands around. "...we have a real problem here. The entrance to the mine was here," he said, as he led them through the rubble, "but it's completely sealed with rock and debris. The gryphons have been hauling it away as fast as the men can fill their carts, but they can't dig the way dragons can."

Emily spoke up. "Certainly both Esmeralda and Harriet will move as much as they can. Do you know if anyone is still alive in there?"

"I'm hoping Lucy will be able to answer that question. That's the most important information we need. This mine runs underground for several miles in three different directions. We have no idea how extensive the collapse is or where any miners might be. Can you help, Lucy?" Baron Geldsmith added, sounding desperate.

Lucy said, "Of course I can help. I'll do the best I can. After all this is one scenario that William has been training me for. How long has it been since the collapse?"

The baron looked utterly exhausted. "It's been six hours," he said. "We're losing hope that there's enough air in the tunnels to sustain anyone."

Lucy moved slowly over the area, walking in ever-widening circles. She was having trouble distinguishing the thoughts of the rescue workers from those of any victims. "Could you ask your men to take a short break and step over into an area away from the mine? I know speed is important, but I'm getting a lot of chatter, for lack of a better word. It's hard for me to tell if there's anyone below ground."

The baron nodded. "I understand," he said, then ordered a temporary halt to the digging.

Lucy and Harriet slowly circumnavigated the area. Everyone seemed to be holding their breath. After about five minutes, Lucy and Harriet moved more quickly toward the north, along what must have been one of the mine tunnels the baron had indicated. They walked for nearly a mile. Lucy relayed what she was hearing to Esmeralda, who, through Emily, told the others.

There are miners alive here. She was quiet for another few minutes, and none of the rescuers said a word. Lucy continued, *From what I'm sensing, there are about twenty miners alive right below us. Some are badly hurt. One man has better telepathic abilities than the others, so I'm trying to communicate with him. He says the mine tunnel has collapsed on both sides of them, and the air is getting very stale. I've instructed him to have everyone stay put and not talk.*

Baron Geldsmith, Emily, and Gregory raced to Lucy's location. The baron yanked out his map of the mine. He and Gregory consulted and asked the mine supervisor, Joshua, for suggestions about how to access the miners without further collapse.

A plan was quickly drawn up, and the baron brought his men and gryphons to work in the new location. Lucy was interested to see that Oswald was there and able to move in more closely and dig better, because he didn't have wings to hamper him, even though he, like all gryphons, lacked the dragons' long talons. Esmeralda quickly demonstrated that she could dig the fastest, so everyone else was delegated to remove whatever she dug.

Lucy and Harriet kept walking around the mine area. After about a half-hour, she called out again. "There are ten miners still alive in this tunnel too!" Quickly some of the rescue workers were dispatched to the new location.

When Lucy and Harriet found another pocket of survivors, the baron said, "We need more dragons to help. Can you ask Hans?"

Emily said, "I did when Lucy found the second group of miners. William and Jake should be here any minute. That'll give us two strong browns."

Sure enough, just as she finished saying this, they spotted the two dragons high above, coming in for a landing. The rescue workers let out ragged cheers.

Lucy hadn't found any more miners, but then Sage startled her. *Let me down. My ears are much sharper than human ears. You've found the pockets with lots of miners, but what if there are isolated miners? Please let me help.*

She's right, said Harriet. *Her ears are better than either yours or mine.*

Lucy carefully removed Sage and let her roam, cautioning her to stay away from the workers, as she could easily be stepped on or buried in rubble without anyone realizing.

Sage walked carefully and slowly, and all of a sudden, Lucy felt someone watching her. It was William. He came over to them and said, "You brought a cat?"

"Not just any cat, William. I was on my way to tell you what happened this morning when Hans caught me first. That's Sage. I can communicate real words to her, and she can communicate back, to both Harriet and me."

William nearly fell over. "Truly? That's amazing."

"I suspect it doesn't happen often, but I'd just moved Sage into our cave when Hans called for the emergency rescue. Harriet and I felt it would be better to bring her with us. She's hunting for single miners who aren't loud enough for Harriet or me to sense. Sage's ears are much sharper."

At that moment Sage broadcast to anyone capable of hearing telepathically, *There's an injured miner below me.*

William, Harriet, and Lucy moved to that spot and called for Gregory to see if it was safe to dig. Once Gregory showed them how to do it, Harriet started to dig. Almost immediately Oswald showed up to cart the rubble away. Lucy was pleased to see how well Harriet and Oswald worked together. One was small and the other wingless, but what a magnificent team they made.

As they dug, Sage kept hunting. Suddenly there was loud cheering as the first group of twenty miners was reached. They were hauled out very carefully. Some were immediately placed on stretchers, as they were badly injured. As the last were lifted from the collapsed tunnel, the leader of the group told the baron that five of his men had lost their lives.

The work continued slowly. Sage found three more pockets that had one or two miners. Many of the rescuers had been there since the collapse eight hours ago, but no one would leave. Some of the Forbury residents had set up tables laden with food and water. A makeshift hospital tent also was erected, and three doctors and five nurses were treating the injured.

The work continued. William and Lucy didn't think anyone really had noticed Sage or realized that it *was* Sage who was moving tirelessly over the entire hillside hunting for isolated miners. Every time she found one or two, she let Lucy and Harriet know, and they called for rescue workers, but she was sure most folks were giving the credit to her and Harriet. Lucy would make sure that changed. Sage refused to stop, but Lucy and Harriet took her some fish strips and milk so she could eat and still work.

Finally Lucy, Harriet, and Sage agreed that everyone who was still alive had been found. Lucy reported this to Baron Geldsmith, who had been keeping a tally sheet. "This is incredible.

Fred—the mine foreman who was in the first batch to be rescued—said there were forty-five men in the mine today. Twenty were rescued in the first tunnel and twelve more in the second, where there were also three dead, bringing the death toll at that point to eight and the rescued to thirty-two. Then you were able to locate three miners, who were alone, and another pair of miners—all alive. We've accounted for everyone."

Cheers erupted from the crowd. The baron called a halt to the operations and had everyone move over by the hospital tents, where he told them how successful they had been. "The eight who died all did so in the initial collapse," he said. "We've been able to remove their bodies. Of the others who survived the collapse, all have now been rescued—all thirty-seven men." Once the cheers died down, the baron continued, "The rescue was accomplished thanks to a lot of people, gryphons, and dragons. We never could have gotten to those men in time without the abilities of Lucy here," he said, as he dragged her forward, "and her dragon, Harriet."

There was another loud round of cheering. Just as the baron was about to continue, Lucy held up her hand. "Those of you men who were by yourselves, I want you to know that it was Sage," she said, as she lifted the cat, "who found you. Her ears are much sharper than ours, and she can talk with us telepathically. We found her today, after she had undergone surgery this morning. She's a true hero."

Lucy noticed astonished looks on everyone's faces, but they rallied quickly and began to chant, "Go, Sage!" at the tops of their lungs. Sage purred happily.

"It has been a day of surprises," said Baron Geldsmith with a tired laugh. "We also want to thank Esmeralda, Harmony, Thunder, and Harriet for their skill in digging. Thanks also to my son, Gregory, for his knowledge of earthquakes and slides, and to our own mine foreman, who showed us where and how to dig. Now I believe there's lots of food! So dig in and relax."

Baron Geldsmith motioned for Gregory and the Dragon Riders to come with him to a tent he had set up as headquarters. As they settled into the makeshift chairs, the baron asked Gregory, "Any ideas about what caused this collapse? I know we've been concentrating on the rescue, but did you notice anything?"

"Not a lot yet, Father," Gregory said. "I brought my own maps along—maps of the volcano and the various fault lines—and this particular mine sits atop a major earthquake fault line. It's a line that runs into Draconia and also through your home village of Cliffside," Gregory continued, turning toward Lucy.

"Did an earthquake cause this?" asked the baron.

"Possibly, or else a strong tremor. Do you know if they used explosives?"

"I asked Joshua when I first got here. He said they used no more than usual," answered the baron. "They'd set off several explosions to open a new area of the mine about four hours before the collapse. Joshua was quick to add that they had taken all the proper safety precautions."

Gregory shook his head. "Father, do you remember when we had to set off explosions to block your army in the pass to Sanwight?"

The baron nodded unhappily. "And we had to dig it all out by hand as our punishment."

Gregory laughed, "Well, I suppose you did think of it that way. Maybe you don't remember, but the explosions we used to block the pass caused the volcano to become less stable. We were afraid that any more explosions might trigger either an eruption or an earthquake. I think that's what happened here."

"But mining is one of our main industries," said Baron Geldsmith. "The miners have always used explosives."

Gregory nodded. "I think we need to study the mines and how they're laid out. This one—I can tell you for sure—should never have explosives anywhere near it. Maybe some of the others could, but here digging by hand has to be the only method used."

"Can you stay in Forbury for a few weeks and help us figure that out?" asked the baron.

Gregory looked at Emily, who answered, "I'll check with Hans, but I'd say you could use us all for a week or two to help with the cleanup, as well as the survey of the mines. And face it—if you have an earthquake, it could rumble right along the fault lines to *us*. It's in everyone's best interest to investigate what's going on."

"Thank you," the baron said. "You may all stay with me on my Forbury estate. There's plenty of room. Let me be sure everyone here has what they need, and we'll call it a day."

— 20 —

MINE SURVEYS

Baron Geldsmith showed them around his Forbury estate. It wasn't a castle like the one he owned in Draconia, but it was very large. He showed the dragons into a sizeable paddock and told them to make themselves at home and that if they were hungry, they were welcome to feed from his herds. Then he showed Emily and Gregory to one bedroom, William and Jake to another, and finally, Lucy to a third. Each bedroom had its own bath, and Lucy wasted no time in getting into the expansive bathtub, which was filled with steamy, hot water. Sage watched from the bathroom counter, indicating that she had absolutely *no* intention of getting wet.

Once Lucy was cleaned and dressed, she headed down to the living room, where the others joined her. The baron took them to his office, where he had maps on all the walls. He and Gregory immediately went to the map that showed the location of all the Forbury mines. Gregory unrolled his map of the volcano and fault lines and placed it on a nearby table so they could all compare the two.

After a few minutes, Gregory said, "It looks as if only the collapsed mine and this other one here..." He pointed with his right index finger. "...are near the major fault line. There are some minor lines radiating out from the main one, but those aren't really an issue unless we have a major disturbance. Even those smaller lines are far enough away from your mines that they shouldn't cause an interruption in the mining."

"That's good to hear," said the baron.

"All the same," Gregory said, "I recommend that explosives be the absolute last resort in any of the mines when hand tools simply can't cut through."

"I understand. I'll pass your recommendation on to King Alfred. Now what about the mine that collapsed today and the other one near the fault line?"

"I can't emphasize strongly enough that explosives never can be used in either of those two mines," Gregory said forcefully. "If they can be mined with hand tools, that would be OK, but if not they should be shut down."

"If today is any example of what could happen, I'd say you're absolutely correct. If it hadn't been for your quick response," the baron said, including all of them in his gaze, "we could have lost forty-five good men today."

"We need to find a way to examine that fault line," Gregory said. "I realize dynamite is too dangerous to be used anywhere near it, but how damaged is the line as a result of today's collapse? Does anyone have any ideas?"

No one said anything for the longest time. Finally Lucy hesitantly spoke up. "From your map it looks like there are several steam vents close to the fault line. Could they be of any use in checking the fault line?"

Gregory thought for a moment. "Not directly, at least as far as I know, but we could walk the steam-vent line and look for any fresh breaks in the surface of the land. We also could ask anyone living close by if they felt any tremors."

Emily said, "We could split into two groups. That way we could cover the ground more quickly."

Baron Geldsmith said, "While you're doing that, would it be possible for the dragons to help us clean up from today's disaster so we can see whether this mine can be reopened?"

"Certainly, Baron," answered Emily. "Why don't we eat dinner and have an early night? Tomorrow William and Jake can start to move along the fault line from the mine toward Draconia, and Thunder and Harmony can start right away on the mine cleanup. Gregory, Lucy, and I will head into Draconia, which is about—what?—an hour's distance?" She looked at Gregory for confirmation, and he nodded. Emily continued, "I can then send Esmeralda back to help you as well. We'll keep Harriet. I have a sneaky feeling that more of Lucy, Harriet, and Sage's special communication skills may come into play. How does that sound?"

Everyone agreed that the plan was a good one. As they all had dinner, Lucy was very quiet, and she headed off to bed right afterward. She and Sage crawled into the giant bed, but it took Lucy a long time to fall asleep. As all the plans were made, she had realized she would be walking directly through Cliffside tomorrow, since it was located right on the major fault line. That meant she would be going past her father's dairy farm. She tried not to worry, especially since she'd have both Emily and Gregory with her. Exhausted from the day's activities, she finally fell asleep.

It was early next morning when everyone got up, ate breakfast, and headed out according to last night's plan. They stopped first at the mine, where Gregory briefed William and Jake more fully on where to go and what to look for. "This will probably take most of the day, but with any luck, we'll meet you by evening, and we can call the dragons to take us back to my father's. Good luck."

With that farewell, Gregory and Emily mounted Esmeralda, as Lucy vaulted onto Harriet, with Sage in the saddlebag. They took off for the Forbury-Draconia border.

As Lucy had feared, they stopped just outside Cliffside. After they had landed, Gregory said, "I think our best bet is to check the area of the last major earthquake. The epicenter was about here," he said, as he walked to the edge of the town.

Emily agreed, and after she sent Esmeralda back to the mine collapse to help there, she joined Gregory, Lucy, Harriet, and Sage. As they walked through town, they examined the ground closely. They stopped at a couple homes and asked whether anyone had felt any tremors, but no one said they had.

"Of course you realize the mine collapse happened a few hours before dawn, so most folks probably would have been asleep. That always lessens the chances that they would feel anything," Emily said.

Gregory sighed. "Very true."

Lucy tried to keep a clear head and not think about how close they were coming to her father's farm. Once they were out of town, she tried to sense any life under the earth's surface. She got Sage out of the saddlebag and asked her to try as well. At first they didn't find anything, but as they moved farther into the fields, Sage and Lucy both sensed moles. *I'd be happy to dig them up*, said Sage, as she licked her lips.

No, answered Lucy. *We just want to figure out if they've been disturbed lately.*

Spoilsport, complained Sage, but she was happy to do as Lucy suggested. After they had walked for about a half-hour, Lucy reported that the moles seemed to be untroubled. Gregory took that as a good sign. They continued for nearly another hour, when Lucy's old home came into view. Gregory, who didn't realize where they were, said, "Why don't we ask over there?"

Emily, who did know where they were, said quickly, "No, not there." She looked apprehensively at Lucy. "Let's move on before we're seen."

Gregory looked puzzled, but Emily whispered, "Tell you later," as she moved forward quickly.

However, they weren't quick enough. Lucy's father charged out of the house, waving a shotgun and screaming at them. "Get off my land! You're trespassing, and I don't want any Dragon Riders around here." He raised his gun and shot at them.

This time Lucy wasn't so lucky. She stood between Harriet and her father to protect Harriet. The shotgun blast caught Lucy in her right upper arm. Harriet let out a cry and shot fire back at Eugene. She deliberately missed him, but she cut it as close as she could to scare him.

Eugene was so crazy with anger that he didn't even jump. Gregory was about to run over to him, but Emily said, "No, don't. Please get Lucy up on Harriet, and let's get out of here."

Gregory grabbed Lucy firmly, but as gently as he could, he placed her on Harriet's back, then told Harriet to get Lucy to safety. Harriet was in the air and out of gunshot range before Eugene could reload.

"You two get out of here also, or I'll come after you!" shouted Eugene, as he raised the gun again.

Gregory and Emily ran for it, snatching up Sage as they passed her. They caught up with Harriet in a shady glen just past the dairy farm. Gregory lifted Lucy down, and he and Emily examined the wound. The concern in their eyes was evident. This wasn't a flesh wound. "It looks as if the bone is smashed," Gregory said.

Emily nodded. "Lucy, can you make it back to the mine on Harriet if I wrap the wound and strap your arm to your chest? We need to have a doctor look at you right away. I don't want to wait even long enough for Esmeralda to reach us," Emily said.

Lucy was crying, but Emily thought it was more from anger and sadness than pain. Lucy answered, "I think so. Harriet would never let me fall...even if I can't hold on."

Emily was surprised to hear Sage speak to her. *You do what you need to do. Harriet and I will get Lucy to the doctor as fast as we can. We'll keep her safe. Why did she have to be so foolish as to try to protect us?*

Emily smiled. "OK, Harriet and Sage. She's all yours. I've already sent for Esmeralda. We won't be far behind you. I've also contacted William and Jake. They'll have doctors standing by. Good luck to you all."

Harriet sailed into the air. Lucy thought she might lose consciousness from both the pain and the loss of blood, but Sage sang to her the entire way to Forbury. Lucy had never heard such a beautiful voice, and she realized even in her pain that Sage was singing the lullaby Lucy's mother used to sing to her.

It took Harriet about an hour to get to the mine, even with favorable winds, but as soon as she landed, people who were eager to help surrounded her and Lucy. Both Jake and William were there. When Emily had called telepathically, Thunder and Harmony had rushed to pick them up so they could be there for Emily. Thunder and Harmony were now back at the mine cleanup, but Jake and William were at Lucy's side. Jake carefully lifted her off Harriet as the dragon knelt as low as she could. As William walked beside them, Jake carried Lucy into the hospital tent, where two doctors and three nurses were waiting.

Jake placed Lucy on a table, and the doctors examined the wound on her right upper arm. One of them asked, "Can you tell me how she lost her hand?"

Between clenched teeth Lucy muttered, "Earthquake."

Jake and William took turns explaining, since they, along with Emily, had been part of the rescue team that had traveled to Cliffside after the quake. Jake concluded by saying, "There was no way to save the hand, and her arm also was badly damaged, but the doctor at the time thought there were enough nerves still viable as well as blood flow that it was worth trying to save the arm. That's why they amputated at the wrist."

William went on, "Her father removed her from our hospital right after her surgery, so she received no physical therapy. When she finally returned to Havenshold six years later, she had to have a minor surgery on the scar, which had healed badly. Emily told me then that the doctor was amazed that the arm was still healthy, although not as healthy as he would have liked."

"Thank you both," replied Dr. Evans. He looked grave and turned to Dr. Lewis. "Shall we consult over there?" he said. Dr. Lewis nodded, and the two walked away.

William and Jake tried to distract Lucy as the nurses cleaned her arm. The doctors returned about fifteen minutes later, but their faces were grim enough that both Jake and William realized they had bad news.

Before the doctors could begin, Sage jumped up on the table next to Lucy and cuddled into her left arm. Dr. Evans was about to remove the cat when the nurse shook her head. William and Jake both pleaded with their eyes to let Lucy keep Sage for the moment, so Dr. Evans said nothing. He didn't know where it was coming from, but suddenly he heard the most beautiful singing. William and Jake also looked surprised and then glanced down at Sage. Soon the singing became a duet, and they realized that Harriet was joining in. Sage and Harriet were trying to calm and reassure Lucy.

Dr. Evans finally spoke. He looked right at Lucy and said, "I'm really sorry, but your arm is so badly damaged...and it wasn't truly whole in the first place. We have no option but to remove it completely." Lucy was silent and unmoving. Dr. Evans continued, "Do you understand, Lucy? We're going to have to amputate your arm."

Lucy finally looked him in the eyes and said, "I understand."

The nurse prepped the arm, and the Dr. Lewis administered several pain shots as well as some sedatives. Lucy didn't seem to notice. She was focusing on the beautiful singing. Dr. Evans thought that everyone seemed calmer because of it. Not everyone could hear Sage's singing, because she did that telepathically, but everyone could hear Harriet's beautiful voice, as she chose to sing out loud in a gorgeous alto voice.

Finally Dr. Evans had to ask that Sage be moved so he could work more efficiently. Before anyone could grab her, Sage hopped up on Harriet, who had worked herself completely into the tent. No one suggested that they leave. William and Jake stayed at the head of the table, holding Lucy's left arm above her head so she couldn't move it, and at the same time stroking her forehead. Dr. Evans was fast and accurate. When Lucy whimpered, Harriet sang louder. Dr. Lewis followed right behind Dr. Evans. In record time the stump was sewn shut and bandaged.

Dr. Evans stood back from the table. "I wish I could have those two," he said, as he nodded at Harriet and Sage, "at all my surgeries. Not only did they calm the patient, but they calmed us."

Thankfully Lucy was drifting off to sleep. Dr. Evans and Dr. Lewis motioned to Jake and William. "I imagine you'll be wanting to get her back to Havenshold and familiar surroundings as soon as possible. I encourage you to wait at least twenty-four hours so we can be sure there are no complications. I know Dr. Brian, and he's excellent. If we can just make Lucy stable for travel, she can heal at home."

Emily and Gregory walked in. One look at Lucy was enough to confirm their fears. Emily sobbed quietly and turned her head into Gregory's shoulder. Gregory glanced up at Emily's brothers and William and said, "What kind of evil man could do this to his own child?"

Jake answered, "I suspect Hans and Clotilda are going to have a lot to say. Can we get Lucy back to your father's for tonight? Dr. Evans doesn't want her leaving for Havenshold for twenty-four hours."

"Definitely," Gregory said. "But I'm not sure how to move her."

Just then Oswald walked in. He nodded first to Harriet then to the others. *I would be honored if you would allow me to carry Lucy. One of you could walk on each side. I guarantee I am known for my absolutely steady gait, even in terrain like this.*

And so it was that Lucy, propped up on Oswald, whose back was even broader than Harriet's, with Emily on one side and William on the other, moved slowly to Baron Geldsmith's home. The others went ahead to alert the baron, except for Harriet and Sage, who walked in front, singing the entire time.

The baron was ready for them, and Lucy was soon placed in a bed on the first floor. Dr. Evans and Dr. Lewis had given her heavy doses of pain medication and a sedative, so Emily believed that Lucy would sleep through the night, but someone would stay watch with her all night long, just in case. Of course Sage wouldn't leave her side.

As they were tucking her in, they heard a strange scratching noise. Before anyone could say anything, Harriet had entered the bedroom. Emily looked quickly at the baron, afraid he would be upset about the damage Harriet's talons had done to his wood floors, but Baron Geldsmith merely said, "I'm sure glad I made my doorways extra wide so that Oswald could come in easily and I am also glad that you are a small dragon, Harriet. Lucy is certainly lucky to have you. Make yourself comfortable."

Emily, Jake, William, Gregory, and Baron Geldsmith left the room, knowing that Lucy couldn't have better nurses, and if Lucy needed anything, Harriet or Sage would be sure to let someone know.

Out in the dining room, as they were having dinner, Gregory explained what had happened. Everyone was horrified.

The baron said, "What a crime. You all must get back to Havenshold with Lucy tomorrow as soon as Dr. Evans and Dr. Lewis say that it's safe for her to travel. Don't even worry about the fault line right now."

Gregory thanked his father. "Oh, I forgot. Before this nightmare, Lucy and Sage managed to contact some moles in the fields."

Emily, Jake, and William nearly choked on their food as they said in unison, "Moles again?"

Gregory smiled, glad that something could distract them all. "Yes, you know Lucy and her moles. Anyway, according to Lucy and Sage, the moles are perfectly content and haven't felt any disruptions, so I think we can safely say that the tremors that damaged the mine were local and not indicative of a major quake."

"I'm glad to hear it, although that information certainly wasn't worth the price Lucy paid for it," said the baron.

— 21 —
THE RETURN HOME

Emily walked into the room where Lucy was sleeping. If the entire situation hadn't been so tragic, she would have laughed. Lucy was lying on her stomach on one side of the bed, with her left arm swung over Harriet, who had managed to get her head and front half of her body onto the bed. Sage was sleeping in the center of Lucy's back. As Emily walked in, Lucy turned her head to look at her.

"Is it morning?" Lucy asked in a rather weak voice.

"Yes," Emily said. "It's time to get you up and ready to see Dr. Evans. Can you sit up by yourself? I'm not sure how you managed to get onto your stomach."

"It was the only way I could lie down and still hold Harriet. Plus I'm a stomach sleeper," Lucy said.

"How about if I get Gregory to lift you up and into that comfy chair over there?" Emily asked, pointing toward the corner of the large bedroom.

Lucy agreed, and Gregory came in and easily lifted Lucy off the bed as soon as Harriet had stood up. He gently carried her to the chair and set her down with only a small whimper from Lucy. "I'll leave you ladies so Lucy can wash up," he told them.

Emily helped Lucy into the bathroom, because Lucy was still a bit wobbly from the sedatives she'd taken last night. "You get yourself washed, and come out when you're ready. Call if you need any help. I think the baron is making breakfast," Emily said.

As soon as Lucy was ready, they all headed into the enormous kitchen, which had a large table and enough chairs for everyone. There was even room for Harriet in the corner. Lucy sat in the chair closest to her. Sage hopped up on the table and gave a look that said, *Just try to move me.* Everyone smiled. Baron Geldsmith was carrying a heavily laden tray with more food than Lucy would have thought possible. "I made my famous cinnamon rolls," he said.

"They're incredible, folks. Trust me," Gregory added.

Everyone sat down and dug in. Baron Geldsmith even provided Sage with a bowl of milk. Lucy was pleased that she could eat the rolls easily and thought that the baron probably had prepared something that wouldn't be difficult for her to eat. After the first bite, Lucy realized how hungry she was.

Soon everyone was full, and the tray was empty. Just as Jake and Gregory were starting to clean up, Dr. Evans walked in. He saw Harriet in the corner and did a double take, then looked at the baron, but the baron just smiled as if he always had a dragon in his kitchen.

Dr. Evans got to work examining Lucy and was pleased to see that the bandage had only a hint of pink on it. "I'm not going to change this dressing now. Lucy obviously isn't bleeding more than what we would expect. She also, thankfully, has no fever." He turned to Lucy, "Are you up to flying home?"

"Yes," Lucy said firmly, although her voice shook as she spoke.

"It's the best place for you, and if you take it easy, you should be fine. I'm going to give you another twenty-four-hour pain shot, which should help."

"OK, but no more sedatives," Lucy said. "I hate being drugged."

Dr. Evans laughed. "Deal."

As Dr. Evans finished up with Lucy, the rest of the riders packed up their belongings and prepared to head home.

Emily asked Lucy, "Would you want to fly on Esmeralda with me? Gregory could—"

Lucy shouted, "No!" before Emily could finish her sentence. "I have to be with Harriet."

Emily said, "I understand. I know you're safe with her. No dragon ever loses a rider."

The riders went outside and loaded the dragons. Sage was placed safely in Harriet's saddlebag. Then Harriet knelt as far down as she could so Gregory could carefully lift Lucy onto her back.

The flight back to Havenshold was uneventful, and they made it in just three hours. As they came in to land in the central courtyard, Lucy spotted Hans, Amy, Nurse Beatrice, and Dr. Brian.

As soon as Lucy was standing, Dr. Brian and Nurse Beatrice tried to hustle her into the hospital, but Lucy absolutely refused. "I won't be away from Harriet." She couldn't help crying.

Amy stepped in before Lucy became hysterical. "Don't you think that if I stay with Lucy and you check her often, you could tend to her in their cave?" Amy asked Dr. Brian.

Lucy looked at her with grateful eyes.

"It's most irregular," Dr. Brian said, but Nurse Beatrice, who had worked with Lucy over the years, nodded.

"Dr. Brian, I think we can make an exception in this case," Nurse Beatrice offered. "Amy has raised six children. She has enough experience to know what to watch for. Lucy will be more comfortable there and therefore will heal faster if she's happy."

Dr. Brian hesitated then said, "So be it, but if you need any treatments that I can't do easily in your cave, you'll return here. Understood?"

Lucy nodded. She knew Dr. Brian was sounding sterner than he really was. Amy went with Lucy, Harriet, and Sage to Lucy and Harriet's cave. Amy tried to get Lucy into bed, but Lucy insisted on being in Harriet's nest. Amy agreed, knowing it wasn't unusual for dragons and riders to sleep together, especially through their apprenticeship, and Lucy had graduated just four months ago.

As soon as Lucy was settled, semi-reclined against Harriet, Dr. Brian and Nurse Beatrice arrived with all their paraphernalia and got to work.

As Dr. Brian changed the dressing he said, "I'm so sorry, Lucy, but Dr. Evans and Dr. Lewis did do an excellent job. From their report it was clear that your arm couldn't function with the additional trauma."

Tears streamed down Lucy's face, but she said nothing. She merely nodded to let Dr. Brian know that she understood. He continued, "If you need anything, please let us know. Nurse Beatrice will stop by several times throughout the day, especially for the first few days, but you can reach us anytime." Lucy nodded again.

Nurse Beatrice looked at Amy. "You know what to watch for. Let me know if anything seems odd. Meanwhile keep her eating and drinking."

"I will," Amy said. "She's one of mine after all." She squeezed Lucy's good shoulder.

As soon as they left, Hans walked in. "Is this Grand Central Station?" Amy asked with a grin.

Hans returned the grin then looked right at Lucy. "I'm so sorry, Lucy. This never should have happened."

Lucy said sarcastically, "There's no stopping *fatherly* love." The tears started again.

Hans looked flustered but then said, "I hope you know you have real fatherly, motherly, brotherly, and sisterly love now. You're a member of our family, and we all love you."

Amy looked up, surprised that her eldest had spoken so openly and firmly, but she smiled and nodded at him to let him know he'd said the right thing.

Hans continued, "I've taken evidence from both Gregory and Emily. I've read the report sent back by Baron Geldsmith's doctors. I've talked again with Gretchen about the incident three years ago when your father shot at you. I've passed all the information on to Clotilda. She and Matilda will be here shortly to render their decision. Just know that you're safe now and in a place where you are loved and honored." He took a deep breath. "Oh, quite aside from this heinous tragedy, Baron Geldsmith also sent a report regarding the mine collapse. You saved a *lot* of lives with your talent for sensing thought patterns, Lucy. I understand that Sage was a hero as well." He looked down at the purring cat in Lucy's lap. "I'm out of here, so you can rest. I'll be back with Clotilda and Matilda sometime this afternoon. Until then just rest and let Mom look after you." Hans said his goodbyes then left the cave.

Lucy was very quiet. Finally Amy asked, "Can I get you anything?"

Lucy burst out, "Will they let me keep Harriet now that I'm an even bigger cripple?" She was sobbing in earnest now.

Amy sat on the cave floor next to the nest and put her arms around as much of Lucy as she could without hurting her. She said softly and gently, "You and Harriet have a bond that no one could *ever* break. I know your father screamed hateful things at her hatching, and I know Hans was confused about the protocol, since you hadn't been chosen as a candidate, but trust me, the issue was *never* about your qualifications or abilities. Harriet made her selection. She felt so strongly that I think she would still be in her egg if you hadn't come down to the hatching pit. That egg would have grown and grown with Harriet inside. She made it very plain to one and all that she'd have you or she wouldn't hatch. No one had ever seen that happen before. It makes your bonding even stronger and more special."

Harriet spoke aloud, "I'd like to see anyone get between us. Even Baron Geldsmith knew better than to say anything when I scratched his floors last night getting to you."

Sage, not to be outdone, said telepathically so all could hear, *Don't forget me! I'm here now too. We're all going to stick together.*

That broke the tension, and Lucy calmed a bit. "All I could think of was that my father had ruined things for me again. I've wanted to be a Dragon Rider all my life, but with my hand gone, I gave up hope. Then you and Todd fostered me, and life was good again, but when Harriet chose me, it was like...the heavens exploded. I couldn't go on without her."

"All riders understand that bond. Now just relax. No one is going to take Harriet, and Harriet won't move an inch from your side. Try to sleep. I'll be right here."

Lucy felt better, and she was happy that Amy was there. With Sage gently singing telepathically again, Lucy relaxed and finally fell asleep.

— 22 —

GLOTILDA'S JUDGMENT

When lunchtime rolled around, Amy was pleased to see Gretchen walking into the cave with lunches for three. Lucy woke up and saw Gretchen but didn't know what to say.

Gretchen covered any embarrassment on Lucy's part with a cheery greeting. "I thought you two might be hungry, and I figured inasmuch as you managed to get yourself in a mess again..." She smiled as she looked at her friend. "...that you deserved some cave service."

She handed a covered dish to Amy then sat down on the floor next to Lucy and opened both her own dish and Lucy's. Don't worry," she said, looking at Harriet and Sage, "I brought snacks for you as well."

Gretchen helped Lucy find a place to balance her dish, since it was obvious that Lucy wasn't moving out of the nest. Lucy was amazed that Gretchen could handle everything so nonchalantly, as if it were no big deal that she had just lost her arm. Lucy knew Gretchen cared about her. She had seen the look of pain that had flown across Gretchen's face when she first had walked in, but Lucy appreciated the fact that her friend was treating her just the way she always had.

As soon as everyone was settled with their lunches, Gretchen said, "Sure is lucky we managed to get neighboring caves again, isn't it? We can look out for each other."

Lucy could have hugged Gretchen. "Yeah," Lucy said, "as if you ever need help."

"Hey, that's not fair," Gretchen said. "You know I never would have gotten through my classes, and neither would Ruby, if you and Harriet hadn't helped us. We may *look* good," she said, pretending to simper, "but we know we aren't the brightest pair here at Havenshold. You've always supported us."

Lucy smiled. "Guess so." She returned to eating, noticing that Gretchen had cut everything up for her. *My right arm may not have been a lot of use, but it was sure better than nothing,* she thought.

Before Lucy could start to worry again, Gretchen was chattering on about something that had happened to one of the new riders. "Would you believe he was heading to the kitchens to get food for him and his baby dragon, and he tripped and fell right into a tub of dirty dishes? I think this guy will win the Mr. Clumsy Award for his class. At least neither of us got *that!*"

When Lucy had finished eating, she snuggled back into Harriet's side and was content to listen to Amy and Gretchen chat about all the goings on at Havenshold. Amy asked Gretchen about her life at Cliffside, and Gretchen told several amusing tales of life in her mom's café.

As Gretchen was finishing a story about how her mom had handled a drunken customer, Hans and Clotilda walked in. Matilda also managed to find a spot in a cave which was designed for only one dragon at a time. Gretchen saw them and said, "I'd better get these dishes back to the kitchen. See you later, Lucy," and out she went.

Clotilda pulled up a chair from the other side of the room, and Hans went to sit on Lucy's bed next to his mother. Once they were settled, Clotilda began, "I've looked at all the evidence—and there is a lot over the years—of your father's treatment of you and his growing isolationism in general. None of us wanted to burden you, but after your father's outrageous behavior at Harriet's hatching, Hans and I felt it was time to look into your background and try to find out what had happened."

Lucy looked up quickly at both Hans and Clotilda but didn't say anything. Clotilda continued, "Hans told us the story that your father shouted at him about losing the love of his life to the Dragon Riders. We followed up with that, even though it was absurd to think that a twelve- or thirteen-year-old could be that much in love." She sighed. "Turns out we did find a record of this girl named Mary. She was an orphan who had been fostered in your father's house when both she and your father were about five years old. They grew up together, and apparently your father was very attached to her. She came here as a Dragon Rider candidate, but she wasn't selected. You know that candidates who aren't selected are given a choice of remaining here and picking another apprenticeship or returning home. The records show that she refused to go home—she was *afraid* to go home in fact, saying that Eugene had already tried to claim her as his future wife and his intensity and determination were frightening—and she took an apprenticeship as a cabinetmaker. She became a skilled craftswoman and eventually married another cabinetmaker from Granvale. They're now living there happily and have five grown children.

"So, even as a child, your father was unbalanced. When Mary didn't return home, he eventually married your mother, but we found something unusual there as well. Emily has been going to Cliffside over the years—ever since she found you—to gather information. Marta was a big help to her in her investigations."

Lucy looked startled, her eyes opening wide. "Marta? What did she know? She never told me anything."

"She told Emily that she would have told you when you reached eighteen, but before then she didn't see how it could possibly help you, so she stayed silent and tried to watch out for you. In any case," Clotilda went on, "from a very early age your father had a reputation for cruelty, so none of the women were interested in marrying him. However, your mother had gotten pregnant, but her boyfriend was killed in an accident. When Eugene got wind of that, he offered to marry her, and she agreed, as she felt she had no other options."

Lucy exclaimed, "So my father *isn't* my father?"

"That's what Marta said, but rather than just take her word for it—as all this obviously happened a long time ago—we decided to run blood tests. William and Jake were very helpful in this regard. Hans had asked them to escort your father out of Havenshold after the hatching, and Eugene was already in a temper. It wasn't hard to provoke him into a fight. William ended up with Eugene's blood on him, just as he and Jake had planned. Nurse Beatrice immediately took it to find out the blood type. We already had your type on file from your surgery right after you got here. We type all riders in case of emergencies, and fortunately it was easily determined that your father could *not* be your biological father."

Lucy looked confused. "But...no one ever said anything, and when my mother was alive, my father wasn't like how he is now."

"According to Marta, your mother was a wonderful woman. She was able to keep your father saner than he has been at any other time in his life. She even got him to show you some attention, because your mother doted on you. When she was killed—and to add to his loss, she was killed saving you, who wasn't even his child—he lost what little grasp he had on his sanity."

Lucy shivered, and Sage snuggled closer. "Does anyone know who my real father was?"

"No," said Clotilda with a frown. "Your mother had a secret affair, but before they could get married, he was killed. We know very little about him. He wasn't from Draconia, but other than that, we know nothing. The fact that he fathered you helps us understand a bit more about Eugene, and Emily's fact finding also uncovered Eugene's instability from an early age.

"And now we get to yesterday. Obviously Eugene cannot be left to stew on his own. His shooting you was unconscionable. He must be punished. Hans has done an excellent job of documenting everything for me: all of Emily's information, Marta's testimonials, the evidence of his attempt to shoot you and Gretchen—everything, including what happened yesterday. On the basis of this information, I've made my decision."

Clotilda paused for a long moment. Lucy was shaking.

"Many people, including riders, tend to forget that dragons have a powerful magic. We don't need to use it often, but in cases like this, it's an invaluable resource. Eugene is very sick, and it would be wrong to execute him, but he can't be allowed to endanger you or anyone else. He already has stopped going into town. In fact he never leaves his farm. He scares off anyone who comes onto his property. Therefore my judgment has been that he will stay on his farm for the *rest* of his life. I've placed wards around the twenty acres he owns so that he cannot leave and no one can enter. This dragon magic is so strong that people passing the farm won't even know it's there. It essentially will be invisible. Once a year I will designate a rider to check on the wards for me and to check on Eugene. It's unlikely that he will change, but it's only right that we verify things annually, just in case. He has enough land and resources to be self-sufficient, as he himself has proven over the last six years. When he finally dies, the wards will dissolve, and the land will become yours to deal with as you see fit. This is my judgment. Neither you nor anyone else will ever be threatened or harmed by him again. Do you have any questions?"

Lucy looked stunned. There was so much to absorb, but right now she just felt a big sense of relief. She hadn't realized how much fear she had been carrying inside her. She said, "No, I have no questions, and as my father...I mean, as Eugene has removed himself from society already, it seems a fitting answer. He may never even realize the wards are in place. Thank you."

"Now, if I may, I'd like to clarify a few things for you," Clotilda said kindly, and Lucy looked up at her. "I hear that you've been worried that you might lose Harriet."

Lucy nodded.

Clotilda smiled. "I enjoyed your aerial dance at your graduation. It was obvious that you were out to prove that you are just as capable as a rider with two hands."

Lucy blushed. "Yes, I didn't want any more discussion—not that there had been any with my fellow riders," she added hastily.

"But you remembered the hatching when there seemed to be a question about your bonding with Harriet, and that was understandable. In your aerial graduation dance you set out to prove that the decision at Harriet's hatching was the right decision. You wowed the audience, and your telepathic communications were phenomenal. That was what impressed me the most—and the other riders, I might add. We have lots of riders who do stunts and so forth, but we don't have anyone who can communicate as you do. Hans also shared Baron Geldsmith's report with me, and there are thirty-seven miners who wouldn't be alive today if it weren't for you and Harriet."

Sage added, *And me!*

Clotilda and Hans laughed and Matilda snorted as Clotilda said, "Yes, and you too, Sage. My point is that Lucy is the one who brought you all together. Sage, I suspect you are more than you seem...but we'll let William and Lucy figure that out. I'm just very thankful that you found your way to Lucy and Harriet. Now back to you, Lucy. It's going to be hard to adjust to the loss of your arm. The physical adjustments will be difficult enough, but the psychological ones will be tougher. Remember how many of us care about you, and how important you are— arm or no arm. Enjoy your true family, whom I know are hovering outside here again waiting for me to leave. Heal fast! And by the way, May sends you her best wishes as well."

Clotilda turned to Hans, "Did I forget anything?"

Hans smiled, "Nope, I think you gave us all enough to think about for a while, especially Lucy. We'd better let the rest of my family in before a riot breaks out."

Clotilda laughed and gave Lucy a pat on the top of her head as she turned and left with Matilda. As soon was they were out the door, Robert, Michael, Jake, William, Emily, Gregory, Hannah, and Todd rushed in. It took a while to find spots for everyone. Those who hadn't seen Lucy since her return got to sit closest to her. Emily grinned at them all and then said to Lucy, "See what it means to be part of a big family?"

Lucy just smiled, but that was enough for them all.

— 23 —

LUCY'S INTUITION

After two weeks Lucy's stitches came out, and she no longer needed a bandage. Amy had returned home after the first week, once any danger of infection had passed. Lucy and Gretchen were becoming even closer friends. It was easy to feel embarrassed when you needed someone to help you dress and eat, but Gretchen never made her feel like a cripple. Lucy wasn't sure how Gretchen managed, but she treated Lucy as she'd always had, and without seeming to, Gretchen just did things naturally, always seeing a need before Lucy became flummoxed and then smoothing it over. Lucy didn't know where she would have been those first few weeks without both Amy and Gretchen.

Other folks popped in all the time, but they also had other tasks, so they couldn't be with Lucy as much. Gretchen had convinced Hans that she needed to be relieved from her other responsibilities so she could help Lucy adjust, and Lucy was glad Hans had agreed.

Once Lucy's bandages had come off, Lucy and Harriet spent a lot of time out in the fields, practicing mounts and dismounts. Lucy's balance was off, and it took a lot to get used to not waving both arms during a vault. Lucy remembered Oswald, who had been born without one wing. He was every bit as much of a gryphon as any other, even if he did look a bit like a lion with a strange head. Lucy knew that Oswald's other wing had been amputated so that he would have better balance, but she felt that she could compensate and learn a new technique if she just worked at it hard enough. For the first three months after her amputation, she felt as if her arm were still there—a kind of phantom sensation—which didn't help her adjustment, but that gradually faded.

As she had done when she had lost her hand, she developed various ways of coping, figuring out her daily tasks so she could do things without help. Nurse Beatrice had been wonderful with physical therapy, and this time there was no added scar damage, because she was treated properly. Lucy had even been fitted with a prosthetic arm which she could use when needed, but she found it awkward and difficult to work with, so most of the time she didn't wear it. She was beginning to realize that in many ways, she was glad that the arm was finally gone. Oh, she missed being able to do many small things, but ever since the loss of her hand in the first earthquake, that arm had been weak and fragile. The doctors were right that it wasn't a healthy arm. Losing it was rather like cutting out the last damaged part of her, so that she could now fully heal. While she would never have a complete body, she would have a sound and healthy one. And her job and her passions were not affected. She didn't need an arm to communicate telepathically or to work on an earthquake early warning system. Amy and Hannah sewed clothes that were easy to manage one-handed. Jake and Sylvester took pride in manufacturing various aids to assist her, such as a clamp on her desk with a holder for books or papers. And most importantly, her bond with Harriet was even stronger. Lucy was amazed at what Harriet was teaching herself to do with her talons, so that she could act as a second arm in many situations, such as holding onto papers so Lucy could write without having the paper slide or spearing her food with a fork so Lucy could cut it. Even Sage got into the act by bringing Lucy small items and generally helping out. They made an odd but effective trio.

A month after the incident, Lucy resumed her duties with William and Sylvester, but it took a full six months before she felt like her old self.

Lucy walked into William's office on a hot summer day and said, "I think it's time I got back into the fields to check the fault lines."

William hesitated. "Are you sure?"

Lucy nodded. "I'd be a fool if I thought I could do it alone—I may never have that ability again—but if I could have an assistant, I'll do just fine."

William smiled, relieved she wasn't proposing a solo adventure. "Did you have anyone in mind?" he asked with a laugh, as if he had no idea whom she would suggest.

Lucy blushed. "I'd like to take Gretchen and Ruby." Before he could say anything, she added, "I know they've been floating around from one task to another, and nothing has clicked for them. Gretchen is as comfortable around me as I am around her, and Harriet and Ruby like each other. Plus Ruby hasn't objected to Sage. I think it would be a good fit."

William laughed and held up his hands in mock surrender. "I get it," he said then thought, *I get it better than you know He and Jake had already figured out that Lucy and Gretchen loved each other even if they hadn't realized it yet.* He pretended to think hard before saying, "What you say makes a lot of sense. Gretchen and Ruby make a lovely pair, but they haven't found a niche they like or where they fit. Hans keeps moving them around, and they do OK, but it's nothing where they really feel they're making a difference. This could be just the ticket for all of you."

"Thanks, William," Lucy said. "I don't know that I'll be able to teach Gretchen any communication skills, but if nothing else, she can help me with daily tasks. I figured we'd head out tomorrow, going down to Cliffside and working our way back, if that's all right."

"You're OK with that?" William asked.

"Yes. I am," Lucy said with a newfound confidence.

The next morning the five of them headed out—two riders, two dragons, and a cat that slept serenely in Harriet's saddlebag. They landed outside Cliffside two hours later. Lucy decided they should walk along the fault line so she could hear the moles underground more easily.

Once they got into town, Lucy couldn't hear much at all. Marta came out of the animal clinic and gave her a hug. Gretchen's mom insisted they stop by for lunch. Mr. Jones wanted Lucy and Gretchen to speak to his students. It was a most pleasant day but not terribly productive. Once they left the town proper, they continued. Lucy listened carefully but didn't hear anything unusual until they were several miles out of town. Suddenly she and Sage stopped.

"Did you hear that?" Lucy asked Sage.

"What?" demanded Gretchen, before she remembered that she had to be quiet.

Harriet listened as well. *I don't think the moles are happy here. They seem to be stressed and trying to move away.*

Lucy and Sage both agreed. They all walked slowly. Soon Ruby said, *I feel something. I'm not sure about moles, but there's a sense of unease, as if something bad is coming.*

Gretchen was beginning to feel left out, but then she realized that was silly. She wasn't here to listen to moles but to help

Lucy, and she liked that a lot. She tripped as she was walking and said, "What was that? I thought I felt the ground move."

"You did," answered Lucy. "It was a very slight tremor that most people never would notice. We've been through a bad earthquake, so we're more sensitive. Let's keep going until dark and see how far this sense of unease goes. Then we'd better report back to William and Gregory."

They did as Lucy suggested, and they discovered that the feeling of unease stopped about five miles out of town. After that everything seemed normal. "I'm not sure what this all means," Lucy said. "If an earthquake were coming, I think the unease would run the full length of the fault. Of course we couldn't hear in town, but there wasn't any indication of problems on the other side of town."

"And you haven't felt this before?" Gretchen asked.

"No, but I haven't checked this close to town before. I don't know if this is normal or not. Let's head back to Havenshold and see if Gregory can help."

Gretchen and Lucy went directly to Gregory's office as soon as they returned.

"We went out to check the fault line today," Lucy told him. "I figured we'd be out for several days, just getting a feel for the ground around the fault, but when we walked above the fault this side of Cliffside, we found that the moles were trying to move. They were very unsettled, and their fear levels were rising. This sensation only went on this side of the town for about five miles. After that it was normal, and it was normal on the other side of town as well. Plus Gretchen felt a very slight tremor."

"Can you show me on my map?" Gregory asked.

Gretchen stepped up to the map before Lucy could get there. "It was from here to here." She pointed without hesitation. Both Lucy and Gregory looked at Gretchen in surprise. "What?" she asked. "Did I say something wrong?"

"No," answered Gregory, "but most folks can't find things that fast on a map."

"Oh, that," Gretchen said dismissively, with a wave of her hand "I've always loved maps. It's no big deal."

Lucy hugged her and said, "You silly woman. Don't you know that cartography is a very prized skill?"

"But it's so easy. It isn't difficult, like volcanology or telepathy."

Gregory said, "Did you ever mention this talent of yours to Hans?"

"Nah," Gretchen said. "It's not important."

"Yes, it is!" Lucy said happily. "You'll now be more than chief cook on our trips. You'll be the cartographer. Gregory, is this enough information to alert Cliffside to the possibility of an earthquake? Do you need us to check anywhere else?"

Gregory pulled a map out of his case, a duplicate of the one on the wall. "If the moles are only disturbed for about five miles, I think we're safe for now, but I want you two to check out a few more locations along different fault lines and steam vents. Can you go back out tomorrow? It might take several days, but I'd like you to check these locations." He marked about a dozen spots on the map. "You'll need to be in exactly the right spot," he reminded them.

Gretchen said, "Easy peasy," as she rolled up the map.

"I think we've found your talent," Lucy said with a smile.

Lucy, Gretchen, Harriet, Ruby, and Sage left early the next morning. It took them the better part of three days to check all the spots Gregory wanted, but it would have taken a lot longer if Gretchen hadn't been there to read the maps. They made a powerful team. Ruby was beginning to learn what to listen for, and Harriet was pretty good at hearing the sounds, even if she couldn't pick up all the feelings. Sage was even stronger with sounds and slightly better with feelings, but it was Lucy who could practically *speak* mole.

As they listened at the twelve spots Gregory had asked about, they began to see a pattern. The spots where the moles were most apprehensive lay closest to Cliffside in a circular arc. The farther away they got, the happier the moles were.

After three days of hard work, they headed back to Havenshold. Gretchen had recorded their findings meticulously on Gregory's map, and when they showed him, he was extremely impressed with their field skills.

"I notice," Gregory said, "that you developed a key to record the data, Gretchen. Excellent work. That makes it easy for anyone to see what your results are."

Gretchen looked very pleased with his compliment.

"Let me study this data over dinner, but if my first impressions prove correct, you'll be heading back to Cliffside with an alert in the morning."

After dinner Gregory headed to Lucy's cave and wasn't surprised to see both Lucy and Gretchen sitting on Lucy's bed. "You need to get a couch in here, or a love seat," he teased. The girls blushed as he continued. "You were right. I think pressure is building along the fault line, and it seems as if the center is right in the middle of town. Since the town is nestled under a cliff, the residents need to be warned. Part of the cliff collapsed in the earthquake sixteen years ago, but the rest could go now. If it weren't so costly, I'd have had that cliff cut away, but the residents wouldn't hear of it. You two should head back to Cliffside to hold a community meeting to warn people."

"We'll leave first thing in the morning," confirmed Lucy.

Good to their word, they were in Cliffside by noon. They went first to see the Mayor Gunderson. "An earthquake, you say?" he asked them. "What kind of proof do you have?"

When they told him, he laughed in their faces. "I'm not recommending an evacuation based on some spurious evidence from *moles*. Please, stop wasting my time."

"I was afraid of that," Lucy said as they left. "Let's see if the *Cliffside Gazette* will print anything."

"Good idea," Gretchen said.

They headed to the newspaper offices. The editor didn't give much more credence to their story than the mayor did, but he said he would run a piece in the evening edition as a joke—a "guess what the Dragon Riders are doing now" kind of thing.

Lucy agreed, as long as he printed *all* of their information. She had Gretchen show him a copy of their map, and they made sure he got their facts down accurately. His spin on it as a fanciful tale wouldn't help, but maybe some readers would be able to read the truth between the lines.

After that they spent the afternoon talking to people—at the animal clinic, at the school, with Gretchen's mom, and with anyone else they could find. Lucy didn't find it surprising that those who did believe them were sensitive to animals already. Dr. Penelope made plans to evacuate the clinic to the side of town farthest from the cliff. Marta passed the word along as well. Soon Lucy and Gretchen were gratified to see a mini exodus to the open fields farthest from the cliff. It was only perhaps twenty percent of the population, but it was something. Thankfully a lot of Cliffside residents already lived outside of town, so that helped as well.

When the evening newspaper came out, Lucy heard the laughing at the local diner, but she also noticed some people quietly leaving. She hoped they were leaving town. Lucy and Gretchen helped anyone who asked. Ruby and Harriet were wonderful about letting people load up their household belongs on them, and then the dragons flew them out to the fields. The girls had brought a number of large tents. Thankfully it was summer and the weather was dry and mild, but the tents would help give people a sense of belonging and home.

Lucy and Gretchen got in touch with Gregory, and he asked them to remain in place and continue to monitor the moles at key locations. If, as he hoped, the moles returned to a more normal behavior, the risk probably had passed. If not the evacuation should continue.

— 24 —

EARTHQUAKE

Over the next ten days, Lucy, Gretchen, the dragons, and Sage continued their reports. Each day they found more evidence of moles on the move. Each day the fear levels and uneasiness below the ground grew. By the tenth day, Lucy even had picked up on worms heading to other locations.

Unfortunately, as time passed, many people decided that it was all a big hoax. The flow of people back into the village was considerable. Lucy tried her best to convince them of the increased tensions underground, but most people just laughed.

Lucy was pleased to see that Dr. Penelope and the clinic staff believed her. Marta worked tirelessly to convince folks that what Lucy was finding was the truth. Nancy, Gretchen's mother stayed, but Lucy thought it was more out of love for Gretchen than actual belief. Still they were away from the cliff, and that's all that mattered.

In the early morning on the eleventh day since Lucy and Gretchen had pleaded for the evacuation, the earth shook.

At first there were just a few tremors that most people probably slept through, but Lucy and Gretchen were on their feet immediately. Then the big quake hit. Lucy thought it lasted forever, although it was only seconds. Lucy and Gretchen held each other tightly and watched as the earth opened up practically down the center of town. Then exactly what Gregory had feared occurred. The cliff ripped off above the town and fell right on top of buildings and homes. Large chunks fell deep into the rift.

Dr. Penelope, Marta, and Nancy came over and stood next to Lucy and Gretchen. Dr. Penelope said, "Well, girls, you warned them. You did everything you could."

Lucy didn't find that to be any consolation at all. They sat on the ground and felt the tremors. They were more than a mile away from the epicenter, and there was nothing here that could fall, but the ground shook horribly, and the dragons took to the air in fear.

The quake subsided, and Lucy called Dr. Penelope, Marta, Nancy, Gretchen, Sage, Harriet, and Ruby together. "We don't know if anyone in town survived, but we *have* to look. Harriet, Sage, and I will be able to locate anyone who's alive. Then we'll try to dig them out. The rest of you need to set up whatever first aid facilities you can. Be very careful. Remember, there'll be aftershocks."

Lucy and Harriet sent out a telepathic call for help to any Dragon Riders within reach of their thoughts. Lucy was relieved to hear immediately from Emily, who promised to spread the word and quickly send assistance.

With that assurance Lucy, Harriet, and Sage approached the devastated village. It was a gruesome sight, much worse than what Lucy remembered of the quake when she was seven, but of course then she'd been out of town at the farm when it had happened. She wondered idly whether Eugene had been affected, or whether the dragon wards had kept him both isolated and safe, but there was little time to think of him.

The rest of that long day was a nightmare. At least fifteen dragons and riders were able to assist. Lucy, Sage, and Harriet were instructed to concentrate on finding anyone who was still alive. Once again Sage was remarkable, finding isolated survivors, while Lucy and Harriet were better at finding larger pockets of life. They were able to rescue some animals as well as people. Dr. Penelope had her hands full treating the injured, as the doctor in town was one of the scoffers and hadn't yet been found.

As darkness started to fall, Lucy spotted two gryphons overhead and was thrilled to see they were carrying Dr. Evans, Dr. Lewis, and two very large crates of medical supplies. They quickly found where Dr. Penelope was working.

It was difficult for Lucy to watch as all the bodies were recovered. She felt she should have been able to convince more people to evacuate, but Harriet said, *Even this town, which was hit so badly when you were seven, didn't believe it could happen again. If we'd had a more reliable way of predicting, we may have been able to convince everyone, but folks aren't going to believe moles and worms. It's so sad, but you did all you could.*

Lucy did find some people who had survived under roof arches, strong doorways, and small spaces, where they were waiting and hoping to be found before another tremor smashed them. Sage found a baby under her mother. The mother had been killed, but she had saved her infant daughter. That was nearly too much for Lucy.

Nancy took the baby and put things into perspective for Lucy. "The mother would be *happy* that her baby lived because of her. I know your mom would feel the same way. It's a maternal instinct to save our children. I don't know a decent mother who wouldn't be happy that she'd been able to save her child."

Lucy nodded. She sent a silent thank-you into the universe for her mother then kept searching.

Two days after the earthquake, the village suffered a number of aftershocks, some of them quite strong, and several more badly damaged buildings fell. Lucy didn't think anyone had died in those collapses, which was a good thing especially after all the funerals they had already held. It was beginning to look as if they had found all the survivors they were likely to find. A second orphan, a five year old girl named Grace, had been found in her family's store and now Nancy was looking after her along with the baby. Lucy, Harriet, and Sage were nearly on the far edge of town—the edge closest to Eugene's dairy farm—when they saw someone running toward them. It took Lucy a minute to realize it was Eugene. He was waving a gun and screaming wildly. "I'll get you this time, you monsters!"

Harriet and Sage tried to get Lucy to climb onto Harriet and get out of there, but Lucy was rooted to the spot in horror. Harriet sent out a plea for help. Within seconds, per Emily's instructions, Esmeralda lifted Lucy into the air and out of harm's reach. Harriet picked up Sage in one claw and was ready to take off when Eugene lifted his shotgun and pointed it at them.

Harriet said loudly, "Put that down!"

But he kept advancing. He didn't notice that Jake and Harmony were closing in from behind him. As Eugene set his sights on Harriet, Harmony lifted him off the ground and flung him clear across an open field. Emily, Jake, Lucy, Sage, Esmeralda, Harriet, and Harmony all heard a loud bang. When they arrived on the scene, they saw that Eugene had landed on top of his shotgun, accidently killing himself.

Esmeralda and Emily brought Lucy back to Harriet, and together they walked over to Eugene's body. Lucy looked at the sad excuse for a man and said, "I hope he finds peace now. He never did in life."

Jake put an arm around her and said, "Are you OK?"

"Yeah, thanks to Esmeralda, Emily, you, and Harmony," she answered.

"Clotilda alerted us to the fact that the earthquake had broken the magic wards. If Eugene hadn't been killed, he might have gone on a rampage, since it was an earthquake that turned him all those years ago."

"She was right," Lucy said, as she looked out toward the farm. "I don't ever want to see this place again. I'm going to donate it to the town. They'll need new land on which to settle and build. The farm can be part of it."

After burying Eugene in a grave dug by Harriet, they headed back into town and joined in the recovery efforts. Four days after the quake, the last living victim was found. Falling timbers had trapped a child, but miraculously they had fallen at angles, wedging themselves and leaving a space just big enough for an eight-year-old boy. Thunder moved the timbers, and William reached in to lift the boy out.

"How are you?" William asked.

"It was dark in there, and I couldn't move. I'm hungry," the boy complained.

"What's your name?"

"Scott," the boy answered. "I want my parents."

William took Scott to the central receiving area, where the doctors pronounced him to be in amazingly good shape, with only a few cuts and bruises. Then Marta led him to the food tent and gave him the bad news about his parents, who hadn't survived. She held Scott as he cried and cried. Finally she was able to get him to eat.

Gregory arrived ten days after the quake. He had been studying all the data the riders had kept funneling off to him. He gathered the surviving villagers and spoke to them. "I'm so sorry for this tragedy and your losses. This was—as you know much better than I—a truly serious quake. The records for Draconia go back more than five hundred years, and no quake of this magnitude ever has been recorded." Gregory paused and let his eyes sweep over the dirty, tearstained faces. "Those of you who were here sixteen years ago know that a lesser quake struck then—smaller but still devastating. Your village sits directly over a major fault line, where earthquakes are much more likely to occur and where volcanic activity also could disrupt life here."

"So what can we do?" shouted a woman from the back.

"My recommendation," Gregory said, "is a hard one, but I recommend moving as far away from this fault line as you can."

"Move?" a woman in the front called out. "Where would we go?"

"Do any of you know the village of Chauncey's Creek fifteen miles from here?" Gregory asked. Several villagers nodded. "On my way here, I stopped there to talk to them. They have land where farms could be built, and they'd like to have a bigger population. Their village is much smaller than yours, and they don't have some of the things you did—an animal clinic, a village school, a blacksmith, and so on. I talked to them for several hours last night. From what I've learned, your two villages have a lot in common."

"But *move?* This has been my home for all my life," said an older man.

"I know," Gregory said. "It's hard, but look around you. You've lost nearly eighty-five percent of your population, and all your buildings. A deep crevice is running right through where your town was. I don't mean to be harsh, but I want you to realize how much harder it would be to clear this all and rebuild than it would be to move. The riders would all help to make sure you're safely relocated. Think about it overnight. We'll call for a vote in the morning. We'll help anyone who wishes to relocate, and if you decide against relocation, we'll help you clean up here. The decision is yours."

Gregory moved away from the crowd and went to find Emily.

She updated him on the latest events and recounted the sad story of Eugene's death. "I think Lucy is finding closure, but what a terrible way for that to happen," Emily concluded with tears in her eyes. Gregory agreed and wrapped her up in his arms.

— 25 —

RELOCATION

The next morning all the Cliffside survivors gathered in the center of the evacuation field outside of town. Dr. Penelope and Marta had become the default leaders of the band of about fifty people. Lucy, Gretchen, and all the other riders and their dragons waited at the edge of the field. They would help carry out whatever plans the survivors made. Gregory stood closer to the group, just in case they had questions about the land, but he was silent as the survivors talked.

Dr. Penelope began, "I've been to Chauncey's Creek, and it's a lovely spot. I've been called in a few times over the years to treat some of their animals, so I've seen a bit of the area. I doubt you could say it's even a village, as there's only one central building amid outlying farms. The population is only about a hundred, maybe less. If we all go, we'll significantly boost to their numbers." She looked at the gathered survivors. "I know this is a really difficult decision to make, but look around. I did a head count last night. We have sixteen men, eight children—three of them orphans, below the age of ten—and twenty-seven women. That isn't a lot to start all over with. In addition many of our people are injured, some severely."

Marta spoke up. "What Dr. Penelope has presented is the blunt truth, and we need to hear that. But it doesn't count our spirit. We are *survivors*. We've had to rebuild before, and we can do it again."

There were cheers, and though they were ragged, they were still cheers.

Marta continued, "Do we want to rebuild here, where an earthquake could hit us again? Or would we like to rebuild where there are others who could help and whom we could help in return? Both of our communities are small, and now ours, sadly, is a great deal smaller. Chauncey's Creek has some flooding issues in the winter. And the land isn't great for farming, which is why there are a lot of goats." She was interrupted by some laughter at that comment. "But the residents are hardworking folks like us. I think going somewhere new to start over makes more sense than trying to rebuild with that..." She pointed at the large crevasse and the building debris. "...to have to clean up or look at every day."

Dr. Penelope concluded, "Riders are here to help us with whatever we decide. What's it to be? Let's have a show of hands for those who want to go to Chauncey's Creek."

Hands slowly were raised. Dr. Penelope and Marta counted. Nancy was one of the last, but finally she also raised her hand. Dr. Penelope looked over at the group of riders and said, "OK, looks as if we're going. How do you want to handle this?"

Jake stepped forward. "It's about fifteen miles to Chauncey's Creek, and it isn't a hard walk, so those who are able, I'd suggest packing lightly and heading out. We have rider food packets and water bottles for everyone."

About half the folks started to gather their few belongings before moving toward William, who was handing out supplies.

Jake continued, "For those of you who are walking, don't worry. If you get tired along the way, we'll be flying back and forth, and we can always offer you a ride if needed. Dr. Penelope, do you have anyone who is too injured to be moved?"

Dr. Penelope looked thoughtful. "There are a couple I would prefer not to shift until last, so that I can have something set up for them on the other end, but I think for that short of a distance, they'll be OK."

"Great," Jake said. "We'll be sure you and Marta are in the first group, along with some tents that arrived last night when more riders came to help."

Soon everyone was moving around, gathering their belongings or helping others. Lucy and Gretchen had been put in charge of the children, and Nancy was holding the smallest infant. Lucy suspected that Gretchen's mom would be taking in the three orphans, and Lucy thought that would be a good thing for both the orphans and Gretchen's mom.

Jake and William took off with the first load, and Emily and two other riders left shortly thereafter. Each rider was able to take two passengers with them, so it wouldn't take many trips, especially since nearly half the group had decided to walk.

Lucy and Harriet took Scott, and Gretchen and Ruby took Nancy, Grace, and the infant.

By afternoon everyone had been evacuated to Chauncey's Creek. Dr. Penelope had set up an infirmary in the town hall, which thankfully was large enough for everyone to gather. It was a very large room with wood paneling as well as windows in every wall, giving a light, airy feel to the space. There was a large table in the center of the room and a podium at one end. As soon as they were all present, the mayor of Chauncey's Creek came to the podium speak.

"Welcome!" Mayor Jane said. "We're happy you've decided to make your new homes with us. We'll do all we can to help."

The survivors murmured their thanks. The mayor continued, "Right now you may all stay here at our town hall until you find your way. The riders have promised assistance to us all. I have a map here," she said, trying to unfold it. Marta stood up and offered her help. Soon the map was spread out on a large table, and the Cliffside folks gathered around.

"I've marked the existing farms, and I've also made notes about the surrounding unclaimed lands," Mayor Jane said, "so you can see what kind of lands there are. The ones closest to the creek flood occasionally during the winter months, and I marked them and any swampy land in blue. Then, farther away from the creek, we have some rocky land and then some *really* rocky land." That got a few chuckles from the tired evacuees. "I marked those in orange and red. There's some high-country pasture much farther from the center of our village that folks haven't picked yet, because of the distance. It's five or six miles from here, but it's good grazing land, and I've marked it in green."

"Thank you so much, Mayor Jane," Marta said, as Dr. Penelope came over after settling the injured. "You've gone to a lot of work to help us get started here."

The mayor smiled and said, "We're too small at present to have a real village center, with amenities you folks took for granted, like small shops, an animal clinic, an infirmary, or even a school. You're going to help us with numbers and skills, so that'll be possible. We won't be quite as large, at least yet, as Cliffside was before the quake, but we'll be close. You folks have experience and skills that we need. Seems to me that together we could make a really pleasant place here for all of us."

This brought a round of cheers from the Cliffside group. Dr. Penelope said, "Thank you so much, Mayor, for your kind welcome."

Jake stepped forward with Gregory. "OK, listen up! Everyone is now here. It's nearly dinnertime, so the riders will fix some food while you all figure out how you want to set up this space for now. In the morning those who are ready and able to start looking over the land may do so. As it's only midsummer, you should have time, with our help, to build homes before the weather turns nasty. You pick your spots and clear it all with the mayor." Jake nodded at Mayor Jane. "And we'll bring in supplies and offer grunt labor."

Everyone laughed at that.

Emily spoke up. "Our senior class of riders always needs projects. You've given us a wonderful one for them, Gregory." Two of the riders who had arrived last night groaned loudly but then smiled. They were obviously a couple of riders from the senior class.

Dr. Penelope said, "Mayor, may I ask how much of the land immediately surrounding this town hall has been designated for the village center? I'd like to have my clinic and attached home here, if that's possible, and I know Nancy here," she said, as she ushered Gretchen's mother over, "will want to start her café up as well. Mr. Jones broke his leg in his attempt to rescue a student as well as books from the school, but I know he'll be up and around and looking to get a school running by winter."

The mayor looked very pleased. "I've marked the town center in pink on the map. You can see we even have a crossroads here. The town hall is on one corner. See here," she said, as she pointed, "and we always thought the school would go here." She pointed to another corner. "It might work out well to have your clinic on the third corner and Nancy's café on the fourth—cozy and practical."

Dr. Penelope, Nancy, and Marta nodded. "I'm sure Mr. Jones will be happy with that as well," the mayor said.

The meeting broke up. As the riders prepared dinner, a number of the citizens of Chauncey's Creek came in and introduced themselves. Lucy looked around the crowded room and thought, *This is going to work...but I have to figure out a way to be sure another quake doesn't prove as costly in lives.* With that thought, she went to help with the dinner preparations.

— 26 —

MAPPING DRAGONIA

It was incredible how much happened over the next week. All of the families found new locations for their homes, either in town or in the outlying areas. A few even chose the high-country pasture, since they had lived outside Cliffside before the quake and were more comfortable on their own.

The riders rounded up any livestock from Cliffside that had managed to escape the earthquake, and they were now back with their owners. Nancy took in the three orphans and now seemed happy as could be planning her café and mothering Scott, Grace, and baby June as Nancy had named her since no one knew what name her mother had picked. Mr. Jones was hobbling around on crutches but was directing the construction of his school with his attached living quarters and also making lists of supplies that Jake assured him would be delivered before fall. Dr. Penelope had erected a couple of large tents on her spot so she could begin work immediately while her clinic and residence were constructed around her. Chauncey's Creek was happily buzzing.

Jake gathered the riders and Gregory for a meeting. "After a week I think we have everything started, and everyone has found a spot. It's time for most of us to head back to Havenshold.

You senior apprentices will stay of course," Jake said, smiling at Rupert and his green dragon, Emerald, as well as Margaret and her yellow dragon, Celeste. "You both can reach Havenshold telepathically, so don't hesitate to ask for help or send in your supply lists," he concluded.

With that the other riders mounted up and headed back to Havenshold. They reported to Hans immediately and gave him a complete update.

The next morning Lucy went to see Hans. "I thought I might be seeing you soon. Great work again on the rescue," he said.

"But people didn't *believe* me. I knew something was about to happen, but I couldn't convince the townsfolk to evacuate. Even those who did...after a few days, they returned when nothing had happened. When the earthquake did strike, the fatality rate was enormous." Lucy looked down at her feet.

Hans very gently said, "This is new to most of us, Lucy, and most people don't believe other species can communicate with us or have anything *worth* communicating. Of all the species, they would be least likely to believe in moles and worms having that ability."

"Oh, I know. I've been laughed at all my life—except here at Havenshold—but I'd really like to do more to help. Gregory suggested that if I were able to survey all of Draconia and gather more data, we might be able to develop a warning system," Lucy said earnestly.

"Sounds reasonable. What are you proposing?"

"You've heard, I expect, that Gretchen is an excellent cartographer?"

"Yes," Hans said. "I'm thrilled that she's found her niche."

"Well, I'd like to take four to six months, with Gretchen, to try to map Draconia, finding all the steam vents, fault lines, et cetera, and see how much communication I can develop with the moles," answered Lucy quickly.

Hans thought for a few moments. "There are logistics involved in keeping riders in the field for that long. You could go out for a week at a time and return, but that would require a lot of travel time and make the entire survey take longer. Hmm." He paused while he thought. "You know, this is a really good idea. Don't know why it wasn't done years ago. Let's get Gregory and Emily in on this," he concluded, then sent out a telepathic call to his sister.

Emily and Gregory showed up at Hans's office about ten minutes later. Hans filled them in on what Lucy had proposed.

Emily smiled at Lucy before saying, "That's a big project for newly graduated riders, but I know both you and Gretchen have a special interest in earthquakes."

Gregory was very excited, nearly jumping out of his chair. "This is just what I've wanted to have happen for *years*. Our maps are so limited. We could plan so much better with real data, even things like how to relocate folks when the worst happens."

Hans interrupted, "Hold on, Gregory. I know we need this, and I know it's long overdue, and now that we have Lucy, it's finally possible, but having them out in the field for that long, even in the summertime, requires some fancy logistics."

"Right," Gregory said a bit glumly, sitting back in his chair and looking at his feet.

"Don't worry. I think if you and Emily are willing to be brought into this, and possibly William and Jake, it'll work," Hans said. "Lucy and William have worked together on telepathy for so long that I think no matter where Lucy and Gretchen are inside Draconia's borders, they'll be able to keep in contact with William, at the least, and probably Emily as well. We need riders who are willing to go out once a week to bring them supplies and check on them. Lucy and Gretchen also could send their data back that way, and you, Gregory, could start working on it, refining it, and letting Lucy and Gretchen know what you need."

"I'd do that easily," Gregory said. "That is, if you and Esmeralda would take me," he said a bit sheepishly as he looked at Emily.

Emily laughed. "You couldn't keep me away, as long as Hans gives me leave from training as a future leader."

Hans chuckled. "You're some trainee, but you're right—there may be times when one or both of you will be needed here. That's why Jake and William should be backups or rotate weeks with you."

They all discussed a few more points then left to get ready. Lucy flew out of the office and raced to tell Gretchen. They'd have the summer together doing research and enjoying each other's company.

Three days later Lucy and Gretchen were ready to set out. They had loaded their saddlebags with provisions, and Gretchen had packed a tent and sleeping bags on Ruby. Sage, of course, was riding in one of Lucy's saddlebags, and Lucy had fixed it so that Sage could look out, if she chose, without fear of her falling out.

The summer was wonderful. Lucy and Gretchen took advantage of the lovely weather and worked hard every day. Lucy, Sage, and Harriet all listened carefully for moles and other underground animals. Gretchen took notes of all the information they gathered. Gretchen found that the maps she had gotten from Gregory were accurate for the most part, but many small steam lines and fractures were unmarked. Sage especially was learning to communicate with moles so that they would communicate in return, and that was tremendously helpful.

They had to set up camp nearly every day, depending on how quickly they progressed. Gretchen tried to find camp spots that were more central so they could radiate out from them each day and return. As they refined their search techniques, they became more efficient.

Most nights they never bothered with the tent but instead lay under the stars in their sleeping bags. Lucy and Gretchen became very, very close friends. One night Gretchen admitted that she'd had a crush on Lucy since they were about nine.

"What?" Lucy asked, her heart racing. "Why?"

Gretchen blushed. "You've always been really cute, and I couldn't help admire the way you were able to get such good grades while you were being bullied and had to work and... *everything,*" she finished in a rush.

"But...no one looks twice at me. No one ever has," protested Lucy.

"I have, and I still do," Gretchen said.

"You? But you're gorgeous and fun, and everyone likes you. Why would you pick me?" spluttered Lucy.

"Don't know," Gretchen said with a song in her voice. "Maybe it's your ability to talk to worms," she teased.

"Well, but..." Lucy said, but she got no further, because Gretchen took her in her arms and gave her a long, passionate kiss.

"Wow," Lucy said, when they finally came up for air.

"Yes. Wow," agreed Gretchen.

From then on their sleeping bags were zipped together. Sage told them, *Makes it much easier for me to dodge feet with twice the room.*

Emily and Gregory noticed the change immediately when they came out the following week to bring food and pick up data. Emily gave both Lucy and Gretchen big hugs and said, "I'm so happy for you both."

The summer went by way too fast. They were up at dawn, worked very hard all day long, and had lovely summer evenings and nights together. Lucy discovered that the moles had their own network. After a while, with help from Harriet and Sage, they managed to tap into it. The moles, realizing what the riders were needing, promised to send word through the mole network to Havenshold if there were any changes or worrisome movement along the fault lines or in the steam vents.

Gretchen was having a wonderful time making new maps. She vowed to learn a lot more about cartography when they returned home, just as Lucy was working on communicating with even more species.

Finally, after five months, they returned to Havenshold. The weather had turned from that of summer to late fall, and it was getting too cold to sleep outside.

Gregory was amazed at how much data they had gathered. "It'll take me months to analyze all this. I hope you two plan to help—especially you, Gretchen. I can't believe how much information you crammed onto each of your field maps, and I'm not familiar with all your symbols."

Lucy and Gretchen assured him they would help. Lucy raced off to tell William about the mole network, and he was thrilled. "We need to set up regular listening posts for you, Harriet, and Sage, so that you'll be able to get any updates right away," he said.

Lucy laughed. It had been a sublime summer, but it felt so good to be back home.

— 27 —

FULL CIRCLE

It was a cool, crisp, sunny day. Lucy and Gretchen were sitting on the bench in the backyard at Emily's home. It was the winter solstice, but it wasn't a hatching year, so they were all celebrating with a large family dinner. Lucy and Gretchen had been chased out of the kitchen, on the grounds that new couples didn't have to help. Lucy tried to protest, but in fact she was glad that she and Gretchen got to cuddle on the bench before the others came out.

After finishing the dinner preparations, Amy, Emily, and Hannah came over to the bench to sit with them. All five women were wearing heavy coats to protect themselves against the cold. "Cooking for an army is hard work," groaned Hannah, as the others laughed.

"We are quite a bunch, aren't we?" Emily said.

Amy shouted across the yard, "Todd, don't set the place on fire!"

Todd looked over from the backyard fire pit. "Who? Me? Never," he said with a devious smile, as he added a few more logs to the fire.

Emily laughed. "Leave it to Dad to make a big thing out of a little barbecue!"

"Well, he's getting a lot of help from the others," Amy said. The five women looked over to see Hans, Jake, Robert, Michael, Gregory, and William egging him on. "There's something about fire and men," she said, as she shook her head.

Lucy looked out over the big sandpit, where Harriet was happily sleeping along with Fire Dancer, Harmony, Thunder, Esmeralda, Ruby, Fireball, Fern, and Jupiter. They all seemed quite content, each having dug their own depression to snuggle in. "It's a good thing Todd made that pit so big," Lucy commented.

Hannah laughed. "And it was all *your* doing!"

Gretchen looked questioningly at the others. Emily said, "Don't tell me that no one has ever told you this story."

Gretchen smiled and shook her head. Emily looked at Lucy in astonishment. "You haven't told the love of your life about how you started your career at Havenshold?"

Lucy blushed. "Tell, tell!" Gretchen said, giving Lucy a quick hug.

Amy said, "I think it's my turn to tell 'The Tale of the Moles and the Sandpit.' Once, ten years ago, a scared thirteen-year-old was found in a cave, cold and shivering. She was rescued by a rider and her dragon, who brought her into our family. It was the *luckiest* day of our lives." She smiled at Lucy. "She came out into the backyard, all by herself, before dinner on a day much like this, and sat on this very bench," continued Amy.

Hannah interrupted, "There should be a commemorative plaque!" She ducked as Lucy tried to bop her on the head.

Amy wasn't deterred. "As I was saying, this little thirteen-year-old was sitting on this bench when she realized she was hearing *moles*." She was interrupted again as Sage pawed at the ground and a mole stuck its head up to complain. Amy laughed. "OK, I can see that I'm not going to be able to tell this story properly." The mole ducked back underground. "But it was right here, ten years ago, that Lucy discovered she could sense what moles were feeling, and she found out about the steam vent that runs right under our backyard."

Gregory walked over to stand behind Emily, gave her a hug, and said, "Right. Just when I was starting to worry about the steam pressure in the volcano."

Amy smiled and said, "When Todd found out about the vent, he decided we had to have our very own heated sandpit, not only for Fern and Jupiter but also so you kids would come home more often."

"I tried to keep the project manageable," Robert said, as he and Michael walked over.

"*Right,*" the rest of them said sarcastically.

Robert rolled his eyes and tried unsuccessfully to look aggrieved.

Amy finally managed to conclude, "The rest, as they say, is history, and that's why our ever-growing family..." She looked kindly at Gretchen. "...has its very own heated sandpit with room for at least nine dragons. In addition Lucy's communication career began, and ultimately she developed her earthquake early-warning system, the volcano was calmed, and we have space for everyone."

They all expressed their happiness in their own ways as they looked out at the rainbow in the sandpit—two greens, two browns, a purple, a blue, two yellows, and a red.

"What if one of us bachelors hooks up with a Dragon Rider? What will Dad do then?" Michael asked.

"Make a bigger pit." Todd laughed as he, Jake, and William joined the group.

"Who's watching the steaks?" Amy asked.

"We came over to tell you they're nearly ready. Are you ready for us?" Todd asked.

"Always," replied Amy, linking her arm with Todd's. "Robert, Michael, will you bring the steaks in? Everything else is all laid out."

"Sure, Mom," Robert said. The rest of them headed inside.

Everyone sat down to what was pronounced by all to be a wonderful feast. Amy and Todd looked around the table. They shared a look that said just how lucky they were as everyone began to dig in.

Lucy squeezed up against Gretchen and thought, *It doesn't get better than this.*

ABOUT THE AUTHOR

Daphne Ashling Purpus lives in the Pacific Northwest on Vashon Island with her three dogs and three cats. She volunteers as a tutor at Student Link, Vashon's alternative high school, and is an avid quilter who makes lap quilts—called portable hugs—for anyone who needs a hug. She loves to write both poetry and fiction. *The Egg that Wouldn't Hatch* is her second novel.

CPSIA information can be obtained
at www.ICGtesting.com
Printed in the USA
FSHW021946270320
68567FS

9 780615 763309